A Passion For Tom

Sandra Salinas Newton

Table of Contents

Autumn and Winter 1920

1. First Meeting

When it was over, he whispered in his funny accent to call him 'Possum.' It wasn't much of anything (he had lain his hand briefly on her breasts), but he put his finger to his lips afterward, indicating that she should keep this incident private.

She had been on her way downstairs to the kitchen; he was returning from the water closet at the back of the house. In the narrow, dim corridor, they both had to turn sideways. It was as they were sidling past one another, face to face, that he raised his hand, allowing it to touch her breasts as they moved. He stood still, his hand resting on her, his eyes watching her face. She blushed, caught her breath, and smiled. She moved away, but not before she noted that he'd smiled back.

She hadn't intended to say anything. It was so small a matter. Other guests of the master and mistress had been more forward, one even trying to lift her apron and skirts in the narrow corridor when footsteps coming upstairs from the kitchen startled him. She never said anything about these incidents; she did not intend to jeopardize her position in the household.

Anyway, this gentleman was different: he was an American with an English wife, very young (compared to some of the other guests), and he had the strangest eyes, so pale greenish hazel that in the dim hallway, they shone golden. It fascinated her but frightened her, too.

When he turned to enter the drawing room, he straightened his vest and jacket, tugged at the crotch of his pants, and touched his hair to assure himself that it was perfectly in place. Then, strangely, he looked at the hand he'd lain on her breasts, brought it to his face and took a deep breath. He smiled to himself, cleared his throat, and left her alone in the corridor. "Did you miss me, dear?" she heard him say as he positioned himself behind his wife's chair.

She proceeded to the kitchen with the empty pitcher. When she got downstairs, she set the pitcher next to the sink.

"Fill it quickly and head back upstairs. Some of 'em

prefer to mix their whiskey with water," the cook said, turning to her pots.

"Will you be wanting me to assist at dinner service?" she asked after filling the pitcher and wiping her hands dry on her apron.

"No, the manservants will be serving tonight. All of us women will work in the kitchen only," Cook replied.

She spent the next two hours standing in the corner of the drawing room next to the waist-high liquor cart that the butler had wheeled in earlier. It gave her the opportunity to hear the conversation, although she had to keep her eyes averted (she looked at the carpet), except when someone approached to refill a drink from the cart. That was her chance to look people in the face and ask deferentially, "May I add water?" (Most of the ladies liked to dilute their drinks; the men not so much.) Without seeing faces, the only voices she could identify were the master's, Mr. Leonard, and the mistress's, Mrs. Woolf. He liked to be addressed by his first name, she by her surname, revealing much about their personalities. The only other voice she could put a face to was of the man she'd encountered in the hallway.

They all smoked cigarettes, cigars, or pipes, so the drawing room ceiling was swaddled in gray, heavy smoke. The windows were shut against the early evening November fog, and the lamps were all lit, but the weak bulbs failed to light the room more than dimly. Her eyes teared from the smoke and from squinting in the hazy light.

Someone, a woman, said, "And Ottoline Morell really thinks of Bertie Russell as a good friend." Some in the room snickered.

"As do we," the man-from-the-hall answered slowly, drawing out each word. He was either ignoring or was oblivious to the snickering. "Isn't that right, Vivien?"

"Oh, absolutely, Tom!" she agreed enthusiastically. Then, sighing contently, she added, "Would you refill my drink, Tom, darling?"

"Yes. Anyone else need to be refreshed?" he asked

politely to the room.

There were murmurs of "no-thanks" and "not I," as Tom—as she now learned was his name—walked to the liquor cart and her. He held two glasses in his hands. "Would you mind?" he asked, managing to still speak slowly and clearly despite the cigarette dangling from his lips. He was holding one of the glasses empty toward her.

She looked up. His eyes were more green in this light but still tinged with golden flecks. He was, she noticed now, taller than all of the others in the room, probably 178 centimeters, and thin, perhaps 11 stones. His complexion was pale, and his hair a sandy brown, straight, and combed back with a severe part just left of center. Despite having long ears and a large nose, he was handsome in a delicate way. He had no facial hair, and his thin lips curled ever so slightly upward at the corners. She guessed he was around thirty years old.

She uncorked the whiskey and half-filled the outstretched glass. "Water?" she asked.

"Please."

She added water to the three-quarter mark. "More?" she asked.

"That's quite fine," he answered and smiled. He leaned forward. "You're quite pretty," he whispered. Straightening, he said, a little louder, "Now the other glass, if you please."

He held the second glass toward her. "Just whiskey, halfway, my dear."

It occurred to her that, in this light, his eyes were almost the color of the whiskey she was pouring for him. She was about to tell him that when Mrs. Woolf said from across the room, "Lottie, please tell Cook and Mr. Higgins that we're ready for dinner."

"Yes, ma'am," she said, corking the whiskey bottle.

Tom—the 'Possum'—took a sip of his whiskey. "Excellently poured, Lottie," he said softly and winked. He turned away to return to his wife's side.

She curtsied and headed for the kitchen. By the time she was in the hallway and at the top step, she could feel the redness in her flushed cheeks. That gentleman, Tom, had not just put his hand on her—many men had, many more had tried and been slapped away—but whispered to her, smiled at her, winked at her. He demanded she call him 'Possum,' although she had no idea what the word meant. Was it an American term of endearment? She would have to find out not only about this new word but also about this American. But, for now, he required secrecy, so she would have to figure out how she could learn more.

"Cook, Mrs. Woolf says they're ready to eat," she said.

"Go tell Higgins to get the men ready for service," Cook answered without turning away from her pots and oven.

She walked past the storage room and into the servants' dining room. "Cook says everything is ready, Mr. Higgins."

"Thank you, girlie. Lottie, is it?" he peered at her.

"Yes, sir."

"Well, go help Cook." He turned to the three men seated at the empty table. "Up, men, straighten yourselves. Let's go."

Lottie went back to the kitchen, where two other maids were already placing bowls of food on platters. Cook would point to a pot and then to a bowl, then one of them would transfer the contents of the pot to the bowl and wipe the rim of the bowl clean. The men came in and picked up the trays of food from the trestle table; they disappeared with the trays into the hallway, and the women could hear them walking up the steps.

At the other end of the kitchen, they heard the scraping of chairs from the dining room overhead; the guests were seating themselves for dinner. Presently, a bell rang in the kitchen near the stove. Cook smiled; she had timed the service perfectly.

When they had finished transferring the various foods from the pots and pans to the bowls and serving trays, they brought all the utensils to the sink to soak in soapy water. They would now sit to eat their dinner while the men served upstairs.

When the men were done, the women would reset the table and serve them their dinner.

They sat—four women—Cook, Lottie, and the two temporary maids from the village—to their dinner. They could take their time since the men would be serving food upstairs for at least an hour: soup, fish, goose, salad and vegetables, all followed by a hot dessert, then fresh fruits and coffee. Cook served a hearty stew with leftover lamb and fresh bread; later, the men would finish the stew but also eat the leftovers from the upstairs dinner: perhaps some fish, definitely the rich taste of the goose, reminiscent of roast beef, as well as generous helpings of boiled, herbed potatoes and stewed vegetables.

"This was your first time as a beverage-maid, Lottie. Did you like it?" Cook asked Lottie, ladling some stew into her bowl.

"It was fine," Lottie answered and smiled. "Except for the smoke from their cigarettes and for standing still in the corner for so long. My eyes started to burn, and my feet started to ache."

"You have to learn to excuse yourself," said Mary, one of the older maids. "Just pick up a bottle or pitcher that's half-empty, catch the mistress's eye, and point to it. She'll understand you need to go to the kitchen to refill the thing." Mary smiled. "Walking will relieve the aches."

The other maid giggled. "And what did you think of all the people?"

"There was a strange one there—American," Lottie said.

Cook stopped eating a moment. "And how do you know he's American?"

"Oh, he's got an accent, and I heard Mr. Leonard say, 'Do all Americans believe that?' and the American answered, 'Most of us, yes.' Then, everyone laughed."

"Believe what?" Cook asked.

"I didn't hear that part," Lottie said sadly. She didn't want to admit that she had been daydreaming about Possum's eyes until Mr. Leonard said the word 'Americans' in an impatient way. She'd been taught to always be attentive when on duty.

"So, why is he strange?" Mary asked. "Americans are just like us except that they talk funny."

"No, he was different," Lottie said. She poked tentatively at her stew, looking for the carrots which she liked best.

"Now you'll have to explain what you mean, Lottie," Cook said. She tore a chunk of bread from the loaf and dipped it in her stew.

Lottie would not tell Mr. Higgins what she was about to tell the women; he would disapprove of her narrative. Mr. Higgins, like all of them, believed in the privileges of the employer and that class, but Mr. Higgins also believed, unlike most of the rest of them, that these privileges should not be discussed among the servants, especially if it was a female servant who'd had what Mr. Higgins called an 'encounter,' by which he meant a female servant being touched or handled inappropriately. "Please don't mention this to Mr. Higgins," Lottie pleaded, looking at the group.

"You've had an encounter," Cook said, sighing. She stared sternly at the other two maids. "Not a word, ladies," she warned. They nodded. Cook turned to Lottie. "Tell us."

"We was passin' in the hallway, me to the kitchen and him to the drawin' room," she started, looking from face to face. They looked interested, not disapproving. It gave her the courage to go on. "So, in that narrow space, we had to turn ourselves sideways-like in order to pass." She licked her lips because her mouth felt dry. "Just as we was face to face, he held up his left hand, palm out, like so," she raised her hand chest-high, "and his fingers lingered and brushed gently on my boobies as we side-stepped past each other. He smiled, then put the finger of his right hand to his mouth and winked. Later, in the drawin' room, when I was pouring whiskey for him and his wife, he whispers to me, 'You're quite pretty' in his funny American accent."

"So? We've all—you included, Lottie—had worse. Men

grabbin' at us, tryin' to stick their tongues—and worse things—in us," Cook said. "You may not believe it, but I was young and pretty once, too. With your beautiful curls and your dainty body, it's no wonder more of 'em ain't grabbin' at you. What are you now, nineteen? Enjoy the attention, my girl."

Mary and the other maid nodded and chuckled. They were almost finished with the stew.

"It's not what he done," Lottie protested, " it was how he acted: like it was so wrong, and I shouldn't tell anyone. Like it was a secret between us. Most of 'em," she looked up at the ceiling, indicating the guests upstairs, "want the world to know they'd had liberties with one of us."

"Yes," Mary chimed in. "I would think him an invert if he didn't touch you in that situation." The others nodded. "We all know that men—given a chance—will do whatever they want, 'specially with the likes of us servants, unless they're inverts sniffin' after other men."

Lottie agreed, adding, "So why be so secret-like about it?" She shrugged.

"Especially here at Monk's House," Cook said. "These people, what call themselves the Bloomsbury Set, have no respect for tradition. The master and mistress take lovers—of both sexes—whenever they fancy. All of their friends seem the same, but what's it to us? We've no rights. They're all socialists and bohemians. Just play along, I say."

Lottie smiled and agreed with everything that was said, but inside, she was wondering if he didn't actually care for her. Maybe he *was* different in more ways than just being American.

When the men came downstairs to have supper, Lottie managed to pull one of them aside when he was going to fetch his pipe. "Do you know who that couple—the American and Englishwoman—are?"

"The Eliots? They ain't been here before, though I hear the husband has already visited the master and mistress at Hogarth House in Richmond, London. Why?"

"No reason. They seem younger than the rest, that's all."

"Well, the cabbie who brung them told me he works at Lloyd's Bank, but his wife thinks he should quit and write poetry. He says they argued about it all the way here from their flat in West Hampstead. Seems they have only been married a few years."

After the guests left and the rooms were straightened up, Lottie and Cook retired to one of the out buildings outfitted with beds and a dresser for them; their quarters had been offered to the Eliots. Likewise, Mr. Higgins and the one valet from town were put up in another of the small outer buildings. The rest of the servants walked home to Rodmell, promising they'd be back at dawn Saturday morning.

When she went to bed that night, Lottie couldn't sleep for thinking about Mr. Tom Eliot. *Tomorrow, when I'm doing the cleaning, I'm going to peek into the Woolf's study and look up 'possum' in their dictionary.* She hadn't had much schooling—a kindly parson took an interest in educating her, thinking she might become a nanny although she was working happily as a servant for want of something better (she needed references, which she hadn't got). She tried to keep up her reading with newspapers and listening to the radio with the other servants every night. And they laughed at her sometimes, saying she was putting on airs by losing her Cockney accent. *I think Mr. Tom Eliot might be more inclined to my friendship if I could demonstrate that I was not just a maid.* On that thought, she fell asleep and dreamt of his sad, golden eyes.

Virginia Woolf had written to Tom Eliot in September 1920 suggesting he visit Monk's House to read some of his poems to the Bloomsbury group. His answer, at the end of October, was to suggest a weekend meeting (he couldn't possibly make it during the week since he worked at Lloyd's Bank as a clerk). They settled on the weekend of November fifteenth.

Also present that weekend were Leonard, Virginia's husband, Desmond McCarthy, a well-regarded literary and dramatic critic, as well as Vanessa Bell, a painter and Virginia's older sister, Vanessa's husband, Clive Bell, and Lytton Strachey, a writer and critic. All were curious to meet the young American

Eliot, who was not really part of the Bloomsbury Group, although he professed to admire them. They understood that he was part of the *avant garde* that also included Ezra Pound (the American poet living in Paris) and James Joyce, the Irish novelist. Strachey and McCarthy were invited to stay the weekend at Vanessa's house, just ten miles away, and although Virginia and Leonard offered to put up Tom Eliot and his wife for the weekend, Tom insisted that he and his wife would stay at the Inn in Rodmell and not inconvenience the Woolfs.

When Tom and Vivien arrived (in a carriage driven by a village man), everyone was surprised to see just how young they seemed. Of the entire group at Monk's House that weekend, Virginia, at thirty-six, was the youngest, the "baby" of the group; the average age among them was thirty-eight. Tom was thirty (to be thirty-one in just a few days), as was Vivien. They seemed, to the Bloomsbury Group, a different generation.

After dinner and drinks, Tom and Vivien begged off, insisting they were tired and did not want to oversleep in the morning and miss breakfast at Monk's House. The rest of the guests—the Bloomsbury Group—stayed another hour gossiping about the Eliots.

Lottie had been assigned to tidy up the dining room and then make sure the guests in the drawing room had enough coffee and drinks and their ashtrays were emptied. She attended to her tasks with deliberation.

"He's quite polished and cultivated," Vanessa remarked.

"Ah, but under the surface, Nessa, it was evident to me that he is very intellectual but also intolerant with strong views of his own about poetry," Mrs. Woolf added.

"His wife was awfully quiet. D'you think that means she agrees completely with him?" Mr. Leonard remarked.

"Oh, assuredly. She clearly adores him," Lytton Strachey asserted. "I should have someone hang onto my every word like that!"

"What a pity he is so enamored of those dreadful others: Pound, Joyce, Wyndham Lewis. Perhaps he'll outgrow them,"

Mrs. Woolf said hopefully. "However does he get anything done whilst working at Lloyd's?" She shook her head.

"Well. he promised to read aloud to us some poems tomorrow, so let's see, shall we?" Dermott concluded, standing. "Shall we get off to your place, Clive? I'd like a good night's sleep if you don't mind."

Virginia wondered to the company, "Will his recitation affect the way we read the poems in print? I don't know."

With that, they all rose and said their farewells at the door. When Leonard closed the door, he turned to Virginia and smiled. "Well, Ginia, that was a pleasant evening."

"Yes, but I can't decide if the Eliots were being considerate or snobbish. Why in the world would they choose to stay at that shabby inn in Rodmell over our accommodations? We haven't a mansion here, but it's a cozy, clean little place. I definitely had the feeling it was Vivien who insisted they stay at the inn, but I wonder why."

"Ask her tomorrow at breakfast," Leonard suggested, laughing. "At least now, we won't need to share a room and give up our private spaces." He headed off to his room. "Good night, my love."

Virginia nodded and watched him walk down the hallway and duck into the far room on the left. Her room was next to his and across from the doorway and steps leading down into the basement kitchen and storage rooms. Leonard respected Virginia's discomfort with sleeping in the same bed—even the same room—with him; he was a gentle man and was willing for their marriage to be and do whatever Virginia decided.

2. The Inn at Rodmell

When Tom and Vivien returned to the inn at Rodmell, they asked the host if he would send up a bottle of whiskey and two glasses and add it to their bill; they'd be leaving early on Sunday to catch the only train to London at eleven a.m., so they wanted to settle the bill tomorrow evening if he didn't mind. He offered to hand them the whiskey and glasses right away, and they thanked him, making their way up the narrow staircase to their room, Vivien supporting herself on the walls as she climbed up and Tom gripping the bottle's neck in one hand and holding the two glasses like oversized finger-mittens in the other hand.

"So, dear Tom, what did you think of them?" Vivien asked, falling backwards onto the bed with a soft thud.

"Useful," Tom answered. He turned on the small lamp, opened the whiskey, and half-filled one glass. "Want some?" He held the bottle out toward Vivien.

"No more for me, darling. It will knock me out, I'm afraid." Vivien's straw hat was in her hand, and she flung it like a disc across the room and laughed. Then, lifting each leg in turn towards her chest, she undid the laces of her shoes and allowed them to fall to the floor. "I could use a kiss, however."

Tom, who had been unbuttoning his vest and loosening the knot of his tie, froze a moment. Then, placing his whiskey on the dresser, he slowly turned to Vivien. "Just one, dear," he said softly. The room was small; it took only two steps to get from the dresser to the bed where Vivien lay. Tom leaned down, holding the headboard's edge with one hand for support, and kissed Vivien's forehead.

She reached out and placed her hand firmly on the crotch of his pants. The wool was heavy and itchy in her hand; she wasn't sure if she was actually touching Tom or just the fabric of his trousers. "Mmm,' she said.

Tom pulled himself erect and pushed away from the bed, taking a step backward. "No, Vivien. Not here." He returned to his drink at the dresser. "You know how I feel about public displays."

"Tom, this room is not a 'public display'! No one is here. We're perfectly alone." Vivien sat up, propped against the headboard. Petulantly, she added, "You insisted we not stay at the Woolfs but here."

"It's a public inn, for God's sake," Tom said, his voice almost trembling with anger. "We shan't talk of this further. Do what you need to do to get ready for bed. Tomorrow is an early and big day. The Woolfs, Strachey, Dermott McCarthy, and even the Bells need to be impressed with me if I am to get anywhere with the London literary scene. So we must both be on our best behavior. Get some sleep, and take your medicines. I want you sparkling and beautiful tomorrow." He finished his whiskey and reached for the bottle to pour another.

"And you, Tom?" Vivien asked quietly. She knew, after three years of marriage, the sound of Tom's rage. It always started with the tremble in his voice.

"I'll go downstairs with the whiskey and sit for an hour or so. That should give you enough time to drop off. Sleep well, my darling," he added with a softening affection. "I'll wake you in the morning after I'm dressed." He opened the door and turned off the lamp but stood in the doorway for a moment.

Vivien waited a few seconds, then: "Goodnight, dear Tom."

He heard her get up from the bed, probably to get her nightclothes, he thought. "Sweet dreams." He stepped onto the little landing and closed the door quietly.

Tom's vest was still unbuttoned, and his tie loose at his neck. He went outside into the late November night and found a bench to sit on. He put the whiskey bottle at his feet and leaned back against the wall of the Inn. The sky was quite clear and bright with stars out here in the country, so unlike London nights.

"Can I get you anything, sir?" The host had come round from the back of the house.

"I'll invite you to a drink with me if you fetch another

glass," Tom said, smiling.

"Thank you, but no, sir. Whiskey's not my cup o' tea, so to speak." The man laughed. "But I'll sit with you a bit if you don't mind."

"Of course, of course," Tom said, sliding to one side of the bench. "Glad for the company."

The older man sat down heavily with a sigh. He pulled a pipe from his pocket, tamped down the tobacco in it, and lit up. "It's a fine night. I hope your missus is comfortable."

"Oh, yes, the accommodations are fine, thanks." Tom pulled a pack of cigarettes from his pocket and also lit up. In the darkness, he mostly saw the host's outline rather than his features: an old, doughy face tending to plumpness, skin wrinkled and darkened by sunshine.

"Begging your pardon, you're not English," the host said.

"No, I'm American, actually. Have you ever heard of Missouri? St. Louis?"

"Missouri? Can't say I have. St. Louis? If you mean the saint, then I've heard of 'im."

Tom chuckled. "No, it's the name of my hometown, but definitely named after that saint."

"But your clothes are English," the man observed.

"Yes, I've been living in London for at least three years now." Unconsciously, Tom rubbed at his neck where the stiffly-starched collar had left a red abrasion.

"During the war, then," the man added.

"Yes. I'd hoped to join the U.S. Navy but was rejected, unfortunately." Tom poured himself more whiskey. The bottle was only a quarter full now.

"You're a lucky young man. So many suffered. So many died. Such a shame."

Tom nodded, although he wasn't sure the fellow could see that in the dark. "Assuredly," he whispered.

"Well, I must be off to bed. Always so much to do with an Inn and a farm to run." The man got up. Peering at Tom in the dark, he said, "Have a pleasant rest, sir."

"Thank you," Tom answered, listening as the man walked around to the back of the house. A door opened and shut, a bolt drawn to it.

Tom wanted to be sure that Vivien was asleep before he went back to the room. It was the only way to avoid a confrontation, especially after she had been drinking. They'd been married three years, and Vivien still held to the mistaken idea that she could make him actually enjoy sexual intercourse. He shook his head. She could not, never would. He would commit to the act only when his urges became unbearable and overwhelming. Then, he needed release. That was all. It took only moments; he was, almost immediately after, able to return to his routine, his asexual existence, at least for awhile.

He'd tried explaining this to Vivien, and she'd say she understood and it was all fine, but more often than not, she wanted to cling to him, touch him, curl up in his arms like a pet dog or cat, and it took all his effort to hide his revulsion, his queasiness with that physical closeness. He became quite clever at thinking up excuses (use the W.C., have a cramp, need to make a drink, etc.) to move away and then sit alone and separate.

Tom stood up, stretched, and went inside. He left the empty whiskey bottle on the counter and climbed the steps slowly and quietly. When he entered the room, the moonlight allowed him to see Vivien sleeping, curled in on herself. Her clothing lay in a heap on the floor.

Tom took off his suit jacket, folded it in half, and laid it on their luggage. He sat in the one thin upholstered chair in the room, removed his shoes, and slouched into the chair so that he could stretch his legs out, feet crossed at the ankle. He undid his tie and folded it in half, laying it on the floor next to the chair. He unbuttoned the top button of his shirt and removed the starched collar from around his neck. Folding his hands on his stomach, he sighed deeply and closed his eyes. With any luck, he wouldn't have too much of a backache in the morning.

When he opened his eyes, the room was suffused with dawn, a kind of hazy light in which everything could be seen but not sharply. "Gentle," he whispered, "it's a gentle light." He looked over at Vivien, still asleep, still curled up as if she needed to protect herself. Tom extended his arms and legs in a languid stretch. He wanted to yawn out loud but stopped himself, not wanting to wake Vivien. Quietly, he took his shaving kit, a pair of pants, and a fresh shirt from their valise and laid them on a chair. It had taken a while and a certain cleverness, but Tom had managed, once married, to maintain his propriety in personal grooming. He never washed, shaved, or dressed in front of Vivien—it would be unseemly—so he'd taken to rise early in order to complete these tasks before she was up. At home, it was simple enough to complete his morning rituals alone despite their not being able to afford separate bedrooms as he wanted (as his parents had): he had set up a small portable bed in the hallway outside their bedroom. Here, however, in a small, cramped room at an inn, it took a bit more finesse to attend to these matters while not disturbing Vivien. Nonetheless, it was better than trying to do this in someone's home—too much of a possibility that the hosts or their servants were up and about, affording him no privacy.

Once he'd washed and shaved using the pitcher and basin in the room, he changed his shirt, adding a new starched collar and tie. Then, watching to make sure Vivien didn't wake up, he unbuttoned and pulled off his trousers and underwear. His leather truss, like a complex belt, needed to be readjusted, and he found it easier to just remove it and put it back on. Once released from the imprisonment of the truss, his double inguinal hernias drooped slightly and seemed to grow in size, like two freakish globules of flesh on either side of his penis. He only looked down at the hernias to insure they were 'placed' so the truss would hold them stationary; otherwise, he avoided looking at what he inevitably had to touch—any private part of himself. Finally, he buttoned up his pants, put on socks and shoes, carefully carried the basin, and went downstairs.

Outside, he emptied the basin and took it around back to

rinse it at the water pump. After using the W.C., he returned to the front of the house and sat on the bench with the empty basin at his feet. He leaned back against the wall of the inn and closed his eyes, allowing the first rays of sun to warm his clean-shaven face. He was pleased that he'd successfully passed another night and morning without having to deal with Vivien's demands on his attention.

When they were first courting back in 1915, Tom was simply overwhelmed with Vivien. They'd kissed; he'd even dared to touch her breasts (still fully clothed, of course). He never dreamed of taking their physical relationship any further—she was a lady, and he a gentleman, after all—although there were times when Vivien seemed willing. After three months, and both of them eager to consummate the relationship, Tom proposed. Implicit in the proposal was that their physical desires would only be fulfilled within the bonds of marriage; Vivien accepted readily.

Their wedding night (and subsequent week) set the tone for the rest of their married life. First, when Tom revealed that he was, at twenty-six, still a virgin, Vivien was sympathetic but only after first laughing and making a casual joke of his innocence. Then, in bed, when he awkwardly caressed her and fumbled getting himself inside her, she threw back the covers and said, "Oh, Tom, let me." Reaching to lead him by his erect penis into her, she felt the lump of the hernias. "What's this?" she asked innocently, her fingers on the small bumps. Tom pulled away immediately and said, "Oh, Vivien, it's a very private matter."

"So is what we're doing, dear," she laughed. "Or trying to do." She kissed him, put her tongue in his mouth briefly, then whispered in his ear, "Just do it, please, Tom."

He got on top of her again and, taking a deep breath, with his left hand, led his penis into her. It was barely a moment later that he ejaculated inside of her, and his penis slid out of its own accord. He was embarrassed; this was not how it was supposed to go.

Vivien sighed and said, "Roll off me, darling. I need to get my medicine." She'd smiled at him and looked amused. It was not the only time they'd had sex, but it was hardly different each time they did it, and always at Vivien's instigation. Tom had come to approach it as his marital duty and nothing more; he assumed it would be different with another woman, perhaps one not so experienced as Vivien had turned out to be; he daydreamed about it sometimes.

Tom shivered even though the sun was almost fully above the horizon now. He had been faithful all these three years of marriage, although he suspected that Vivien was not. He had no proof that she and Bertie Russell were carrying on, but his suspicion was enough to convince him that he should—whether for spite or not—find himself an extra-marital partner as well. These people (the so-called Bloomsbury group) were not strait-laced Victorians who would disapprove or condemn such behavior; they seemed almost to revel in it.

His thoughts jumped to that maid (was her name Lottie?) who didn't complain when he'd touched her and who even seemed pleased when he spoke to her. He would make a point to try getting her alone later today. The very idea gave him an erection. He picked up and filled the basin and headed back upstairs.

Vivien was still asleep. Tom quietly replaced the basin on the dresser, unbuttoned his trousers, pulled down his underwear, and let both drop silently to the floor while he slipped out of his shoes and folded the blanket to the foot of the bed. It was perfect: Vivien was on her side, her back to him. He lay gently down next to her and pulled her sleeping body to his.

"Tom?" Her voice was heavy with sleep.

"Lay still, Viv," he said, raising her nightgown with one hand and pulling his erect penis out from between his truss. "This is, after all, what you wanted." He fumbled to find her vagina from behind, then thrust himself in clumsily but assertively.

Vivien sighed and pushed herself closer to him.

It was over in another few moments. As silently as he had come to his wife, he was now slipping away. He stood up. "Don't turn around, dear," he warned, adjusting himself and the unwieldy truss. He dressed quickly. "Shall I go down and fetch you some tea?" Adroitly, he fixed his shirt, collar, and tie, then put on his suit jacket.

Vivien turned onto her back. "That was nice, Tom, but I wish you'd told me so I could have enjoyed it more." She sighed. "Yes, get me tea, but be a dear and first light me a cigarette."

"There's no ashtray in here, Viv, so wash up and dress; we'll go downstairs where you can smoke." He hesitated but then risked an argument: "Sex relieves us of our physical burdens, Viv, nothing more."

Vivien sighed again. "Perhaps for you, Tom."

3. Back At Monk's House

When they arrived back at Monk's House, they found everyone in the dining room talking and serving themselves breakfast from a sideboard: fried eggs, sausage, mushrooms and tomatoes, fresh-baked bread, and even black pudding. One of the serving men stood at a corner of the buffet table near the coffee and tea pots; once a guest took a seat with his or her plate filled, the servant would appear to pour their desired beverage.

Vivien heaped her plate with food and chatted loudly with whoever would listen. "The inn is quite quaint," she said, proceeding to describe its condition and owners in a chirpy, condescending voice.

"We offered you accommodations here," Virginia commented dryly.

"Oh, we didn't want to put you out, and besides," Vivien added a bit waspishly, "Tom and I really value our privacy. Despite being married for three years, we often feel like newlyweds. Isn't that so, Tom?" She held her cup up to the servant. "Tea, please."

Eliot had been putting a slice of back bacon on his plate. "Yes, dear," he mumbled, obviously embarrassed. "You know," he turned to the company seated at the table, "in America, we call this Canadian bacon," holding up the slice of back bacon speared with his fork for all to see.

"It's not from Canada," Clive Bell remarked.

Lytton Strachley snorted.

Leonard Woolf smiled. "It is amusing to note our differences with our American cousins."

"They certainly are incapable of appreciating Tom's talent," Vivien stated.

Eliot smiled weakly and found a seat at the table rather far from Vivien. "This looks delicious," he remarked before requesting coffee and turning his full attention to his food.

"After breakfast, we shall all take the morning air. The

grounds here are quite lovely, particularly this time of day." Leonard Woolf announced.

Everyone agreed to his plan and nodded. Only Tom Eliot noticed that Virginia looked askance at Vivien and then rolled her eyes at his sister, Vanessa as if to confirm her displeasure with Tom's wife. He felt a blush on his ears but continued to eat as if he were having a simply wonderful morning.

Soon thereafter, breakfast was either finished or was too cold to pick at. Virginia told the servants to clear the table and bring the buffet trays back to the kitchen. "Shall we walk?" she suggested and stood up. "Leonard and Tom, come with me," she commanded. "The rest of you sort yourselves out as you wish."

Virginia's sister, Vanessa, looked around the room and smiled. "Let's make two groups, then. Lytton and Mac, you come with me. Clive, be a dear and accompany Mrs. Eliot. Do you mind," she said, turning to Vivien, "if I call you Vivien?"

"I'd prefer it."

"Done, then."

A serving man appeared at the French doors and opened them wide onto the gardens. Songbirds could be heard in the far-off trees, and the buzz of insects gently sounded in the nearby bushes. The eight people walked out onto the dusty path, squinting in the morning sun.

Once outside, the three groups went in different directions, determined not to follow on the heels of one another. So, Vanessa, with Lytton and Mac in tow, headed parallel to the house, intending to circle back to the lean-to conservatory where, once inside, they would be shielded from the mid-morning sun. Clive Bell, Vanessa's husband, took Vivien to the Italian Garden, a paved area of standing ponds and geraniums in giant urns. Clive didn't like to walk and preferred to sit on the stone bench there.

Virginia led Leonard and Tom away from the house along the flower walk, which, even in November, still bloomed with asters, chrysanthemums, and cyclamen. While Virginia was asking Tom to tell her about James Joyce, Leonard ducked into some bushes on the right. When he returned, adjusting the fly and waist of his pants, Eliot asked, "Are you all right, Leonard?"

"Yes, just needed to pass water after breakfast, old man," Leonard replied offhandedly as he got back into step with Virginia. He dropped his arm lightly on her shoulder.

"You—" Tom stuttered, "You urinated there in the bushes?" He seemed shocked.

"I didn't want to walk back to the house and then try to catch up with you two," Leonard explained amiably.

"The plants can certainly use the watering," Virginia added flippantly.

My God!" Eliot answered. He had stopped walking, and when the Woolfs realized he had not kept up, they turned around to face him.

"Tom, what in blazes is wrong?" Virginia spoke to him condescendingly.

"I won't even shave in front of Vivien! I would never do— " he paused for words, "—what Leonard has done here in the open in front of a woman, especially not my wife."

"Why not?" Leonard asked innocently. "She is, after all, your intimate partner."

Tom blushed. "I was raised differently," he said stiffly.

"Come along, let's walk more." Virginia started down the path. "Tom, you really must get over your priggishness," she muttered, her back to him.

"Let's go, Tom," Leonard added.

He hesitated only a moment. He thought himself modern, but these older people had more radical ideas than him, it seemed. Then, Lottie popped into his head again. *I'll bet she's seen things here at Monk's House that are shockingly modern.* Tom was even more convinced that he had to find a way to connect with that servant, if for nothing else than to learn more about the ways of these Bloomsbury folks.

The three groups came back together in the sitting room. It was close to lunchtime, so Virginia headed to the kitchens to speak with Cook about the service. Leonard offered his room to the two men, Lytton and Mac, should they wish to freshen up. Vanessa and Clive said they'd run home to change, and Vivien and Tom were given Virginia's room to rest.

"They are so interesting," Vivien said as Tom closed the door to the room. She sat in a rocking chair and looked around. "What a cozy little room!"

"They are rather more bohemian than I thought, Viv. They really flout convention in many ways." Tom was looking at himself in the small dressing mirror in the corner of the room. He straightened his hair.

"Well, I like it. Out with the old Victorians, in with the new Edwardians!" Vivien giggled and rocked gently back and forth. "And they've given us a room for an hour or so, Tom. Why don't we make use of it?" She smiled wickedly at her husband.

"Vivien, really," Tom answered. He turned to face her. "I'm here to impress these people, not spend an intimate weekend with you." He frowned, then softened. "Why don't you have a nap? I'll go fetch a copy of my poetry from Mrs. Woolf's bookcase to decide what I want for my recitation after lunch." He left the room quickly before Vivien could lodge an objection.

Tom made his way into the hall and found the staircase to the kitchen. When he reached the bottom of the stairs, he said, "Anyone here? I'd like some help, please."

Cook came out of one of the doorways, wiping her hands on her apron. "Yes, sir?"

"I hope I'm not interrupting your work, ma'am," Tom said deferentially. "But I seem to have lost my way upstairs. Could someone show me to the salon?" He smiled innocently.

"Oh, all the men are working outside right now, sir," Cook answered, "and I've some things on the stove that need watchin', so there's only my helper." She shrugged, expecting the fellow to return upstairs alone; this American didn't understand their customs, she thought ruefully.

"Would that be Lottie?" he asked hopefully.

Cook was taken aback. "Well, yes, it would." She wrung her hands.

"Be a dear and lend her to me for just a few minutes, if you please." He put a hand on Cook's shoulder to emphasize his point: "I need her to help me retrieve something from the bookshelves."

It was the gesture of touching her shoulder that surprised Cook enough for her to say, "Of course, sir." She turned to the doorway she'd emerged from. "Lottie, come here."

When Lottie appeared, Tom saw her now in a clearer light than he had last night in the dim hallway or the smoke-choked room. She was lovely: a slight girl of about nineteen or twenty, her light brunette hair reflecting almost-blonde glints from the overhead light. Her eyes were a dark hazel, and her face a pale rose. Her maid's uniform, despite its fullness, did not completely conceal her attractive figure. "Hello again, Lottie," Tom said brightly. "Come upstairs, please. I need your help."

Lottie looked to Cook, who nodded with her reluctant approval. "Certainly, sir." Lottie grinned.

As they climbed the short staircase, Tom put his hand on Lottie's elbow. "I need you to help me retrieve a book from the Woolf's bookcase."

Lottie felt his touch and blushed. "Of course, Mr. Eliot."

They'd reached the hallway and headed toward the salon. "Not in front of the others, but please call me Possum."

"Whatever does it mean?" Lottie wanted to turn to face him, but he gently propelled her into the salon.

"I'll only tell you if you'll meet me later tonight – after everyone's gone to bed – in the Italian garden," he whispered in her ear. Inside the doorway of the salon, he turned her around to face him. "For now, just help me find a copy of my book of poetry that the Woolfs published last year."

Lottie smiled but lowered her eyes. "All right," she answered quietly. She moved across the room to a small side table and picked up a thin book with a brown marbled cover. "Here it is. Mrs. Woolf had me put it out this morning."

"You're a lifesaver, Lottie," Tom said, waving the book happily in his hand. "I've got to practice." He hugged her roughly. "See you later." And he left the room.

Lottie felt the warmth of his quick embrace slowly melt from her. She closed her eyes and sighed, then headed back to Cook, not intending to say a word about what had just happened.

4. The Reading

Tom had decided to read only two poems for the Bloomsbury group until he got a sense of their interest. He'd chosen eleven poems for the Woolf's printing but never talked with them about the poems themselves; it was his second time publishing his poetry, and the Hogarth House press run was small: only two hundred and fifty copies. For today, he picked what he thought were two of his least accessible in terms of meaning; he hoped the audience would feel just a little less intelligent and educated than he, and this would put him at an advantage in any discussion of the poetry.

Back in the room with Vivien, who, in a small chair, was napping in a circle of sunlight coming through the window, Tom realized he really couldn't practice his reading aloud. He settled on simply mouthing the words silently but trying out different postures and hand gestures. It would have to do.

When Vivien awoke, stretching lazily like a cat, she rubbed her eyes. "What poems shall you read, Wonkypenky?" She fluttered her eyes slyly, enjoying the snide nickname she'd given him after his poor first attempt at sex.

Tom shot her a momentary flash of anger, which he quickly swallowed. "Well, Wee, I've decided on the "Sunday Morning Service" and one of the French poems. And, please, dear, stick with 'Tom' when you address me during this trip."

"I would never think of embarrassing you, darling," Vivien answered. "Do you want to practice your reading with me as an audience?"

"No, I think I'll be fine," he said. "I do love you, Viv," he added, grateful that she'd offered to help him with the reading. But he also spoke affectionately to Vivien out of a small sense of guilt that he was planning to secretly meet Lottie later that night.

The dinner dishes were cleared away by eight, and the guests were lingering over the dessert course, the cook's specialty, Apple Cheese, which she had molded, covered with waxed paper and stored in the pantry the week before.

"I believe I've had this when I was a student in Paris," Tom said, spooning a second bite of the dessert into his mouth. "What's it called?"

Virginia's sister, Vanessa, was the first to respond. "We call it Apple Cheese; I prefer the French term, however: Gâteau de Pommes. Ginia's cook makes this excellent version with sliced almonds and sprigs of thyme."

"Isn't it ironic that despite its name, there's not a speck of dairy in it," Clive Bell, Vanessa's husband, added.

"Not at all," Vanessa said. "The 'cheese' part refers to the cheesecloth through which the boiled, mashed apples are strained. But that's why I prefer the French term, *gâteau*, which is simply 'cake,' as a more precise term."

Tom shifted uncomfortably in his chair. "Oh, do you speak French?" He tried to sound casual.

"*Un peu*," Vanessa answered coquettishly.

"I'd say a very *peu*," Virginia commented. She turned to Tom. "My sister fancies herself a European, but Nessa is just an English girl after all."

Tom pretended amusement, but he was actually relieved to hear that Vanessa's fluency in French was largely imagined. "Anyone here speak French, then?" he asked, looking around the table.

There was some mumbling, but all shook their heads. Sensing Tom's relief that he alone would understand his French poem, Vivien bowed her head and smiled surreptitiously at Tom across the table.

"A sloppy language if you ask me," Lytton Strachey intoned. "They swallow the ends of all their words like bloody cannibals."

Most guffawed at his remark. Tom waited for a moment, then said, "Perhaps I can change your mind tonight, Lytton."

"Why? Are we going to discuss international linguistics?"

Suddenly, Vivien blurted out, "Oh, you ought not take

that tone with Tom!" She stiffened her shoulders and lifted her chin. "He's brilliant," she added as if challenging a rebuttal.

Lytton cleared his throat. "No offense meant, I'm sure."

For a moment, the table was silent. Then Tom said, patting Vivien's hand, "None taken."

Vivien withdrew her hand from Tom. "Speak for yourself, darling. I think some people need reminding of your genius." However, when she saw the embarrassment in Tom's eyes, she covered her mouth with her fingers as if to remind herself to be less outspoken, then said, "But, of course, all is forgiven." She smiled demurely.

Tom saw the others exchanging knowing glances: Vivien had again made a spectacle of herself. "Viv has had a long day. I hope my poetry will help you to forgive her."

"Oh, don't spoil the surprise, Tom," Virginia said. "We are all anxious to hear your poetry spoken aloud. But I think we should adjourn to the parlor where we can drink, smoke, and be more comfortable." She folded her napkin and placed it on her empty dessert plate.

"No matter what you prefer calling it," Vivien said as she stood up and pushed back from the table, "that dessert was lovely." She had already forgotten her outburst.

Tom disguised his disappointment that Lottie wasn't serving the drinks tonight. Instead, one of the burly manservants stood stoically in the corner, overseeing and dispensing whatever drinks the guests requested. Within the hour, the room was again hung with smoke from cigars, pipes, and cigarettes. They all thought the atmosphere cozy.

"We're ready for you," Virginia announced. She turned to the others. "Tom has graciously agreed to read us two of his poems tonight. They are, of course, from the volume Leonard and I published last year, called simply *Poetry*, though I daresay the title is deceptively basic." She smiled at Tom.

"Thank you, Virginia. I'm honored, of course. Let me say, before I begin, that I have chosen, as one of the poems tonight, a piece I wrote entirely in French. I apologize if you do not understand French, but I hope you will, nonetheless, understand the sense from my reading."

The gathered guests shifted uncomfortably, stealing glances at one another. "Never mind," Desmond McCarthy insisted, "let's on with it, shall we?"

Tom's demeanor changed. No longer the reticent, seemingly timid and acquiescent guest, he suddenly became assertive, standing up much straighter, his chin jutting out, his shoulders squared. None of the guests knew it, but he was mutating into the amateur actor he'd been as a student in Boston, delighting in recreating scenes from various popular stage melodramas. He cleared his throat. "The first poem is titled 'Mr. Eliot's Sunday Morning Service,' written about two years ago." Tom sat down like a stern schoolmaster, settling deeper into his seat. He took his time opening the slender book of poems in his lap, turning the pages slowly as if searching for something specific. "Ah!" he whispered suddenly, stopping on a particular page. He looked up at everyone and smiled. "Polyphiloprogenitive," he said, the first word of the poem rolling easily off his tongue to introduce the rhyming quatrains of thirty-two lines. Tom held to the poem's rhythm, never stopping for dramatic emphasis or giving a clue about the theme. It was as if he were reciting a familiar prayer, neither passionate nor urgent, just an ordinary devotional for a Sunday morning service, although the accumulation of what was ordinary eventually suggested a sterile hypocrisy hidden, as Tom intended, in obscure and learned references.

"The second poem," he said into the silence that greeted the end of the first poem, "is from a recent time when I thought that writing in French might help me to overcome a bit of writer's block I had in English." A small smile was meant to convey that the ruse had worked. "This is called *'Mélange adultère de tout'*, which, in America, we'd probably translate as 'mongrel.' But, nevertheless. . . ." he allowed his voice to drift off for a moment.

Tom stood up, assuming a posture of great pride and diffidence as he read. The poem was a catalogue of different roles: professor, journalist, lecturer, banker, carefree student, philosopher—whatever the time or place required. His voice conveyed amusement, a sly delight in each line. At the word *professeur*, he pulled a pair of eyeglasses from his pocket and perched them on his nose; at the *banker*, he hooked his thumb imperiously into a vest pocket; at *jemenfoutiste*, he raised an eyebrow rakishly and leered. Each pose, each change of intonation and pitch, caused his audience to smile or laugh, to nod in approval or agreement. Finally, with the last eight lines, which Tom recited meditatively, as if only to himself, the audience was quiet, somehow understanding the poem's underlying melancholy. Tom shut the book quietly, bowed his head once to indicate his performance was over, and sat down.

Only partially joking, Leonard said, "Blazes, Tom, I can't decide which gives me the greater headache: the English poem with words I've never heard before or the French in the language I'm rather unfamiliar with." The others, except Virginia, laughed and coughed as if in agreement. Virginia said quietly in the silence, "Quite remarkable, Tom."

While Tom nodded to Virginia, Vivien blurted out, "Oh, all of you must realize my Tom is quite the intellectual and man of the world." She placed her hand possessively on his shoulder.

"Nonsense," Tom said, snorting. "I apologize that I sometimes like to show off my Harvard education and my year at the Sorbonne. These poems are ample proof of that, eh?" He smiled disingenuously.

"Quite so," Strachey nodded dismissively. It was his way of indicating he had no wish to discuss something he did not understand. "Shall we have a nightcap?"

Virginia looked at Tom and shook her head. When he leaned nearer to her, she whispered, "Why hide your brilliance behind your education?"

Tom blushed but said, "Why, Virginia, whatever do you mean?" He pulled his watch from his vest pocket and briefly noted the time, eleven p.m. Then, "I'm afraid, Virginia, that Vivien will have to return to the Inn for her night medicines; it's very important she stay on a schedule."

"Oh, Tom, how can I help?" Virginia was, herself, not unfamiliar with recurring illnesses, so she was immediately sympathetic. The poetry could be discussed in the future.

"It's nothing new and nothing to be alarmed about, just the usual for us. Staying with a routine, however, is paramount, so may I impose on you to have a carriage take Viv back to the Inn? I'd like to stay a bit, talk with all of you, and perhaps enjoy your garden at night."

"Of course, Tom, I'll see to it immediately." Virginia stood up and excused herself.

Tom moved closer to Vivien and whispered, "Virginia will have you taken back to the Inn, where you can rest until we leave for London tomorrow. I need to stay and talk longer with these folks. They will certainly help advance my career." He squeezed her hand and smiled. "It's best."

Tom knew it was easier to control Vivien when he intimated that his career hinged on her acquiescence to his wishes. Tonight, she'd return to the inn alone because she knew Tom needed the time to advance himself with the influential Bloomsbury people. "I understand," Vivien said, "but you must tell me all about what was said when we get home tomorrow."

Of course, my darling," Tom said. "Don't forget your medicines." It took almost another hour to get Vivien into the carriage. She insisted on speaking to each person individually, so there were various hugs and handshakes before she finally allowed herself to be loaded into the carriage and ridden off into the darkness, to the relief of most of the party.

More drinks were poured, and the conversation turned to desultory gossip about others in the Bloomsbury set. "Are you and Mary planning any trips soon?" Vanessa asked her husband, Clive.

Tom had learned that Clive and Vanessa had an open marriage: he was involved with Mary Hutchinson, the woman who Tom first met through Bertrand Russell. She, in turn, introduced Tom to some of the Bloomsbury people. Clive Bell's wife, Vanessa, had already had an affair with Roger Fry and was now living with the bisexual Duncan Grant and his lover, David Garnett. Still unused to such scandalous behavior, Tom was uncomfortable listening to their gossip. "I think I'll take some air in the garden," he muttered, sensing this a good time to look for Lottie. He slipped out and headed for the Italian Garden, that section to the side of the house containing two large stone urns filled with geraniums. There was a small stone bench tucked into a corner where Tom hoped Lottie was waiting for him.

5. In The Garden

It took him a moment to accustom his eyes to the dark. Especially this late in the year, the night seemed deeper, the stars colder and farther away, so they provided little light. Worse, there was some cloud cover, so the moon was dim. Tom stood a moment, then turning, found himself in the Italian Garden. He noticed a rectangular pool, less than half filled, flanked by a pair of marbled urns planted with late-blooming purplish geraniums. He pinched off a slender stalk and moved forward.

Sitting at the edge of the lone bench was Lottie, turned sideways and looking into the bushes; she had not seen or heard him.

"Ah, you're here!" he whispered as he seated himself close to her. Playfully, he put the sprig of geranium in her hair and leaned in to inhale its fragrance.

"Oh, Mr. Eliot. I thought you weren't comin'. It's a bit late and chilly. I been sittin' here about an hour." Lottie squinted at him in the dark.

"Give me your cold hands, dear," Tom said, taking her hands in his. "And you've already forgotten to call me Possum." He smiled. "Y'know, my mother's name is Lottie, so I couldn't help but like you from the first." He tucked her hands into the underarm folds of his suit sleeves. "Here," he said, squeezing his arms tighter, immobilizing her hands against him. "This will warm you up a bit."

Lottie tried to pull her arms away a little but could not. She blushed. "Oh," she said, feeling the warmth of his body suffusing in her hands. It was a kind gesture, but it seemed to her to be intimate somehow. "P-p-possum," she stuttered, "that's quite fine." She added, "You promised to tell me the meaning of that word."

"Now you must see how easily we get along, Lottie. I can't stay long this evening though. Do you work for the Woolfs only here at Monk's House, or do you travel with them back to Hogarth House in London?"

She wondered if he was avoiding her question about his nickname. "Cook and I work for them permanent-like. Us an' the butler, Mr. Higgins. The rest are what the Woolfs call 'local help', and they hire them when needed, like for parties and such."

"So, will it be possible for me to see you in London on occasion?" Tom asked. He was already plotting future rendezvous. "But how shall I get in touch with you?" He shifted positions and pulled her hands into his lap.

"If you're serious, just send a message to the Hogarth House kitchen. No one needs to know it's from you, sir." She was flustered that her hands were now resting on his thighs. "I mean, Possum."

"Ah, all right, then. You shall eventually get a message from Possum. You should know that the word describes one aspect of me: truly opportunistic omnivorous."

Lottie knitted her brows. She clearly did not understand.

Tom laughed heartily. "It means I try to get the advantage in every situation."

Lottie said nothing, chewing on his words, unable to match their meaning to what little she knew of this man.

"Perhaps, easier for you to understand, I've earned the title because I often 'play possum,' which means I pretend an innocence I have long ago lost." Then, guffawing, he added, "I hope I haven't confused you." He moved closer. "There's one way to keep me from upsetting you," he said, pressing his lips to hers.

Lottie was surprised and almost lost her balance. But she immediately tasted the cigarettes and liquor on his wet lips. She thought it a little unpleasant but was relieved that he hadn't tried to push his tongue into her mouth. It was a chaste kiss, although he pressed hard against her mouth.

He disengaged himself and licked his lips. "You don't have much experience, do you, Lottie?" he asked, looking into her eyes.

"With what?" she asked, confused.

"Oh, men. Also, kissing and touching and such."

Lottie wasn't sure how to answer. Did he want a girl who was more liberal with her affections? She hesitated, then said, a little haughtily, "I've had my share of kissin' if that's what you mean."

Tom laughed. "Your answer and its tone tell me just what I want to hear." He kissed her cheek. "We'll get along famously."

"What are you proposin', then?" Lottie asked curiously.

"An affectionate friendship, Lottie. Nothing nasty." He stroked her cheek.

She wondered what he meant by 'nasty,' but she thought it unwise to ask at this particular moment. "That's easily done," she answered confidently.

"I don't meet many women in your class, Lottie," Tom explained. "I want to know you better, to understand you, to have you understand me."

Lottie felt some apprehension. What was he talking about? She had never heard anyone speak to her like this.

"I'll write poetry and read it to you," he added. He stroked her neck.

"You're unusual if you don't mind my sayin'," she murmured, touched by his caresses.

"We can't meet often, but when we do, it will be quite an experience, I'm sure of it," Tom said and cupped his hand on her chest. "I'll know if my poetry excites you by the beating of your heart," he whispered, gently pressing her breast. "But now," he said suddenly in a much louder voice, "I have to return to the parlor." He stood up. "When you go to bed tonight, Lottie, think of the Possum's hand on you." He turned and walked away.

Lottie sat a few moments longer, watching him retreat into the shadows of the garden. Then, straightening her clothes, she stood and headed for the servants' entrance. "I still have to figure out what 'possum' means," she mumbled to herself.

When Tom reached the French doors of the parlor, he could overhear the voices of the guests inside. He took a deep breath and stepped inside. "Your garden, Virginia, is quite beautiful at night."

"Oh, you should thank Leonard for that. He's the one with the green thumb, I'm afraid. I just look, admire, and get inspired to write." Virginia laughed.

"Speaking of writing, then," Lytton interjected, "are you going to explain to us, Tom, what the bloody hell those poems were about?"

"My God, Strachey," Desmond said, "you're a writer. Are you saying that even *you* don't understand Tom's work?"

Nessa laughed. "At least my excuse is that I'm a painter. Words are bloody troublesome for me."

Lytton responded, "Well, I'm a critic and biographer primarily, not a damned poet."

"And I'm just a public speaker and a prose-writing critic," Desmond added.

They all turned to Leonard Woolf and Clive Bell, who'd been quiet during this exchange.

"Don't look at me," Leonard protested. "I'm a publisher, not a critic or poet."

"You sell yourself short, Leonard," Clive Bell said. "And I'm excused because I'm an art critic, with emphasis on the word 'art' rather than literature." He snorted.

Tom said nothing, pleased that he seemed to have confounded them thoroughly.

But then Virginia spoke very quietly and very thoughtfully. "We are in the presence of someone who will change poetry forever," she said. "I'm not sure how or when, but I sense in Tom an ability to force us to attend to what poetry *does*, not what it says, to attune ourselves to its resonances and textures."

The room was silent. They respected Virginia's opinions highly, but they also often needed more time to fully comprehend her meanings. Tom cleared his throat. "You flatter me, Virginia," he said smiling, but in his hooded eyes was recognition: she knew what he was about, and he appreciated it. Perhaps he should have told Virginia to call him 'possum.'

"I'm not known to flatter so much as to honestly assess, Tom," Virginia answered him, smiling equally.

Lytton asked, "Then poetry, am I to assume, is meant only for a select few, some elite audience?" He had always been, by far, the most pugnacious of the group, willing to argue ideas sooner and longer than anyone else.

Virginia shook her head impatiently. "Nessa, would you please find a leash for Lytton?"

Vanessa laughed. "Lytton, what Virginia is saying is that you don't always need to understand poetry, but you must always *feel* it."

"I could make a rather lurid joke about feeling right now, but I think it would be too vulgar for us and insulting to Mr. Eliot," Lytton complained and lit his pipe.

"Oh, my dear fellow," Tom protested, "I thought you British believed all of us Americans somewhat vulgar." He laughed. "I'm proud to say that I'm one of that group much of the time."

"What do you mean by vulgarity, though?" Dermot asked.

Tom smiled enigmatically. "I don't think many of you are educated enough with either music hall or burlesque, and I too much. You don't spend enough time in public ale houses or on the streets of London. Such a pity that you miss the language of your own country."

"You are quite the proletarian," Dermot concluded, although not in a complimentary way.

"More the *mélange*, the mongrel," Tom corrected.

Virginia stood up. "Where the pedigree is feeble, the

mongrel is strong," she said. "It is now past my bedtime, ladies and gentlemen, so I wish to expel you all from my home. Tom, my man, will bring you back to the Inn to your wife. The rest, except for Leonard, of course, off you go to Nessa's, where you may engage in whatever debauchery you desire. Leonard, will you tuck me in, darling? I will see all of you tomorrow at breakfast."

Virginia had spoken. All quietly did as they were bidden.

6. Back Home in London

A few weeks before they'd spent the weekend with the Woolfs at Monk's House, Tom and Vivien had moved into accommodations at Clarence Gate Gardens in Marylebone; they thought themselves lucky to have found this apartment after Crawford Mansions which they found cramped, unsuitable, and rather disreputable. At the same time, Vivien's father suffered an almost fatal illness so that their return to London was punctuated with frequent visits to Hampstead, three and a half miles away. It was a hectic life: getting accustomed to a new place, assuming responsibility for Vivien's father's care, and adhering to Tom's forty-hour work week at the bank.

In particular, he realized that he needed a life less filled with disasters or inconveniences of one sort or another; he found himself withdrawing deeper into himself, dealing with the external world in dispassionate, mechanical ways. It sometimes gave him the appearance of indifference or, at least, disinterest.

Yet, all these things pointed to their fortunes seeming to improve. However, Vivien's health did not. She continued to be regularly sick with a variety of ailments, so Tom was too often more her nursemaid than her husband. While being administered to him one evening, Vivien asked him about Bertrand Russell, whom they had not seen for some time. He was, they'd heard, headed to China to teach philosophy, and they feared that his outspoken nature would land him in trouble yet again.

"You've known him a long time," Vivien said, almost jealously.

"Yes, longer than I can believe." He saw Vivien's eyes fluttering closed (one of her medicines that made her drowsy) and thought to soothe her to sleep, or at least amuse her, with his account of first meeting Russell.

"I was doing graduate studies at Harvard in 1914 when Bertrand Russell, who was 42, appeared as a visiting professor of philosophy. I liked Russell's assertion that the object of philosophical study was to understand reality, not predict outcomes, but I found the man somewhat distasteful."

"How could you say that about Bertie?" Viv asked, yawning.

"The first impression that Russell made on me was what I reported in a review, that the man seemed a Pan-like figure, vigorous but lustful." He didn't want to upset Viv, so he didn't tell her that Russell's personality attracted and repelled him at the same time; he'd admired Russell's individualism but disapproved of his general behavior. To explain himself, Tom said, "It was, clearly, my first meeting with such a societal outlier, and it fascinated me as much as it frightened me." Tom watched Viv drop into a light sleep. Should I tell Viv that I'd heard about Russell's many adulterous affairs, some simultaneous, and the shameful way he'd treated his wife? No, he decided, because Tom had admired Russell's intellect, he only wanted to impress the celebrated philosopher with his academic observations. Whether because Russell's appointment was temporary, or Tom's ambivalence prevented a stronger connection, the two never bonded until they met again later that year. "And we lost touch when Russell left Harvard."

Tom looked at Viv. "You awake?"

She sighed and said softly, "Tell me more."

"I was in England on a graduate fellowship in October 1914 when, by chance, I met Russell in London. The outbreak of the war had turned Russell's interest to pacifism and away from philosophy. This was a topic on which we disagreed. Nevertheless, Russell generously helped me secure work as a lecturer, a gesture for which I was grateful and which I saw as a new start to my friendship with the famous philosopher." Tom hesitated. "Do you remember when you first met him, Viv?" Tom asked quietly, unsure if his wife had fallen asleep.

"Yes, of course, darling," she answered, the sleep making her speech fuzzy. "What was it? About two weeks after we married? He took us to dinner and dancing as a wedding gift. But he never danced at all." Vivien smiled weakly and put her hand on Tom's arm.

Tom nodded. He did not, however, tell Vivien what he sensed in Russell at that dinner: a distaste for Vivien, as if he thought her slightly vulgar and insincere and, for that reason, ironically, desirable. Truth be told, Tom thought, it was perhaps what first attracted himself to her as well. "The old man would not make a fool of himself by trying to dance," Tom observed. He wanted to add that he hated how she, now a married woman, continued to flirt with men.

But Vivien had now fallen deeply asleep, her head turned to one side and her arms limp on the bedspread. Tom gently tucked her under the covers and quietly slipped out into the dining room, which doubled as his office.

He loosened his tie and removed his suit jacket, draping it carefully on the chairback as he sat down at the table stacked with books, loose pages, and his typewriter. Vivien would be asleep for at least five or six hours, and Ellen, their maid, would not come in until seven a.m., so Tom had some time to himself. His only decision was whether to catch up with correspondence or to work on some criticism for one of the literary journals he knew would pay him for his opinions.

As he was putting a sheet of paper in his typewriter, he noticed his frayed shirt cuff. He looked at it with dismay, remembering that his underwear, too, needed darning; the shirt, however, would have to be replaced. Evaluating this expense along with their other bills, Tom decided that a letter to his mother, including a request for money, would be more fruitful than working on an article.

Tom tried to write home, whether to his immediate family (mother, brother Henry, or Marion, his favorite sister) or to his extended family of cousins, at least twice a week. The mail boats took two weeks minimum to transverse the Atlantic, and then, Tom knew, he had to add at least another three or four days from New York to St. Louis, or even New York to Gloucester, when his family were staying at their summer home. If he wrote often, there would be no great lapse in their correspondence; besides, Tom always needed money, and his letters were usually answered with enthusiasm and enclosures of a bit of cash.

Since acquiring his job at Lloyd's three years earlier (in 1917), Tom believed that he could support Vivien adequately, although not in the manner they'd preferred. Because Vivien was often sick or bedridden, they needed money for doctors and medicines and for a maid to tidy up as well as to shop and cook. Because they had to socialize frequently, thereby supporting Tom's reputation as a writer, they needed ample wardrobes from tailors. Even some supplies like paper were scarce during the war, so prices were higher than usual.

Tom kept meticulous records of their expenditures, a habit he had acquired to demonstrate his level-headedness to his father, and which was further enforced by his position at Lloyd's. It was not in order to spend less or economize that Tom kept such accounts; it simply made him feel more responsible that he'd kept such records. He had been raised in a somewhat upper-class household and was thus accustomed to certain class privileges: decent accommodations, good quality clothes, unfettered access to funds for entertainment, household servants, and frequent holidays. None of these seemed extravagant or unusual to Tom; he saw them as necessary to everyday life and assumed that his family understood his need for their constant assistance in financing these activities.

"That should do it," he said out loud, reading over the letter to his mother. Tom had developed a formula for these letters: start with inconsequential remarks, move into self-praise for publishing and/or financial work at Lloyds, and then request money without specifying what was needed. Make assurances that Vivien wants to meet the family but has been ill and unable to write, and end with some memory of home. In this letter, it was Tom's remembering his mother's expressions of delight when, at age ten, he showed her his one-paragraph description of an engraving that hung in her boudoir, the Bishop St. Ambrose reproving the Emperor Theodosius. His relatively lonely childhood was the repository of many memories that he could call up at will. He sealed the envelope and left it on the sideboard to be mailed tomorrow.

Tom stood quietly behind the open door of his wardrobe and carefully hung up his trousers. His shirt with the frayed cuffs was to be trashed, and his underwear carefully folded and placed in a small pile for Ellen to launder. He put on his pajamas, threadbare at the elbows and knees, and decided that when his mother sent money, he must surely purchase a new set of nightclothes. Vivien preferred to sleep in her underthings, and though Tom thought this somewhat scandalous, he said nothing to avoid arguments. Besides, he slept in a second, smaller bedroom, so it didn't really matter what Vivien's preferences were; they had decided it socially appropriate to sleep separately. While he was settling into the small bed, he had a fleeting thought of Bertrand Russell's experiences with Vivien's nocturnal *dishabille*. Perhaps she was more discreet with Bertrand, his being an older man and a friend to them both, but Tom could not disabuse himself of the notion that, if Vivien had not physically committed adultery with Bertrand Russell, then she certainly had intellectually. Tom was hurt but also relieved: when she was involved with another man (whether actually or imaginatively), she complained less about his reticent sexuality. Tom accepted this as a condition of their marriage.

Settling into the thin mattress and pulling a light blanket over himself, he closed his eyes but retained an image of Vivien lying on her back, her bare legs bent at the knee and wedged between her slender white legs, a male, goat-like figure with almost furry haunches, his head buried in her breasts, huffing lustily. Vivien moans then stretches her neck backward and cries aloud with pleasure. Tom opened his eyes and blinked. He whispered into the dark room:

Comme nous sommes seuls! Comme la vie est triste!

It was the last line of Jules Laforgue's poem, "Triste, Triste"; Tom had memorized the entire poem when he first read it at Harvard. Although he thought the line somewhat melodramatic now, he believed it neatly described much of his life. "And so what?" Tom said into the empty darkness and turned his head to sleep. He disdained such self-pity, a response learned from his Unitarian upbringing.

Two days later, having received some money from his brother (a response to Tom's month-old request), Tom sent Vivien to the dressmaker to order some new outfits for the winter while assuring her that he would himself head to the tailor to be measured for at least one new wool suit and to purchase some shirts, collars, and ties, but he also intended a detour to Hogarth House in Chiswick, about seven miles away; he wanted to meet with Lottie later in the week.

Tom went around to the back of Hogarth House, hoping that the only servants in attendance would be the regular staff—the butler, cook, and Lottie—and Lottie would be the one to answer the door. The Woolfs kept the property tidy; Tom attributed that to Leonard, who seemed more attentive to the household than Virginia.

It was a cloudy London morning, and the air smelled of rain. Tom knocked softly; he frowned because he suddenly realized he had not prepared what to say if anyone other than Lottie opened the door. He removed his hat and pushed his hair back from his forehead with his free hand. He cleared his throat.

Lottie opened the door. "Oh," she said, surprised. She wiped her hands on her apron, then quickly stepped onto the doorstep, pulling the door almost closed behind her.

"How nice to see you surprised," Tom said, pleased that she had been the one to answer his knock and that he had surprised her. Despite her appearance, her apron slightly soiled, her hair tucked back in a bun but coming loose, and a sudden flush in her cheeks, Tom thought her quite attractive and had to stop himself from hugging her. "I haven't much time," he said.

Lottie almost laughed. "Nor I," she answered, briefly looking back into the kitchen, listening for footsteps or an enquiring shout.

"Will you meet me at Holland Road and Russell Gardens on Thursday evening after work? Say, seven?"

"Mr. Eliot!" Lottie blushed even more. "I can't talk with you right now. I won't be done with kitchen work until nine the soonest," she answered in a quick whisper.

"Nine is fine. Don't forget Holland Road and Russell Gardens on Thursday. We shall be meeting halfway between us, Lottie. I look forward to seeing you again." Tom then took one of her hands and kissed her fingers. He smiled and turned away, adjusting his hat on his head. He had no intention of giving her the opportunity to refuse him, and he knew that if he left her standing in the doorway, she would, as a servant, feel compelled to obey his directive.

Lottie, indeed, was left standing, mute, in the doorway. There was no doubt that she could meet him, but should she? What would they do, standing in the road at nine o'clock at night, in the dark, alone? She giggled. It was too cold to actually do anything.

"Lottie?" the cook's voice called from inside.

Lottie shrugged and started back inside the house. He was a strange one, that Possum. She had managed to find out that a possum was a nocturnal animal, formally called an Opposum, that lived in the Americas and in Australia. A drawing she saw reminded her of a rat, but much bigger, with more fur and a long prehensile tail. It was, to her, interesting and dangerous at the same time, and she decided that Mr. Tom Eliot was aptly nicknamed, and it was not surprising that, so far, all their meetings have been at night. "Nocturnal indeed," she laughed. Her spirits buoyed by the unexpected appearance of Mr. Eliot, Lottie called out merrily, "Coming, Cook."

7. With Lottie

"I insist, Tom. You look dreadful, and it will only make my father worry," Vivien said, adjusting her hatpin in the mirror.

"Only if you're sure, Viv. That new hat is quite attractive." Tom smiled wanly, trying to look quite tired despite his energetic anticipation of meeting Lottie in two hours. "I might go round to have dinner at a pub later if I'm feeling a bit better," he suggested.

"Well, since Ellen heated us only some leftovers, and I'll be staying with Papa overnight, you should put something hot in your tummy. I'm sure it will help you to get better." Viv smiled at herself in the mirror and made a last-minute adjustment to her bodice. "Do you really like the hat?" she asked, turning to face Tom.

"It's wonderful," Tom said sincerely. He liked the dark green velvet material wrapped with a flowery silk scarf. The wide-brimmed hat, which Vivien had perched jauntily to one side, shadowed her face, hiding the pallor of her illness. Tom thought she looked seductive, daring, and even cheeky in an attractive way. He leaned forward and kissed her lightly.

"Oh," Vivien responded, "perhaps I should stay home tonight."

Tom blushed. "No. Your father is expecting you, and I really need to coddle myself." He stepped back.

Vivien made a sad face. "What is it you Americans say? 'Raincheck'? Certainly when you're better," Vivien insisted.

"Yes, Viv. I'll give you a rain check. Your retention of American slang impresses me."

"Your insistence on developing a British accent confounds me," she replied. "You'll never get it quite right, Tom, and it confuses people."

"I've told you, Viv, that's the point: I don't want to be pinned down." Tom sighed to indicate that he'd hoped this was the last time he'd have to explain this to her. "Now, off with you.

Have you the money I gave you? Take a motor car; it's too cold to walk." Tom practically pushed her out the door in his eagerness to have her gone.

Once Vivien left, Tom rummaged through the papers on the table, looking for some of the verses he'd written for the long poem he was struggling with. He found two neatly typed pages, folded them, and put them in his pants pocket.

Tom didn't want to look too much the gentleman for his meeting with Lottie, so he'd chosen an old dark gray suit, slightly wrinkled at the knees and elbows, a round-collared striped shirt, and a thin blue wool tie. He combed his hair straight back, slathered with Brilliantine, before he covered his head with a peaked cap. He wanted to look like a typical clerk just out for a date with his girl, not a banker or an academic, although he continued his usual habit of decorating his suit breast pocket with a carefully arranged handkerchief that he purposefully made to look as if it were simply stuffed there thoughtlessly, one of its long edges drooping out and down. When he was an undergraduate, it was Tom's way of distinguishing himself from all the other Harvard men who'd folded their hankies with geometric precision. In Paris, Tom stopped using a cotton handkerchief in favor of a decorative, flower-patterned silk *pochette*, but once he settled in England, he reverted to solid colors, mostly in soft cottons. The idiosyncrasy of having the hanky drape casually over the pocket stuck; it was Tom's small rebellion against the traditional rule of displaying only a carefully folded pocket square, especially at the bank.

He decided to walk the three-plus miles to his meeting with Lottie, hoping to discover a small pub either on the way to or at the destination where they could sit together privately in a corner or a back room. His spirits were buoyed by the idea of seeing Lottie away from prying eyes, and he hoped she would not disappoint him by not showing up. "Okay," he said and smiled at himself one last time in the mirror before he left the house. He enjoyed that word when speaking to himself; it reminded him of home when, as a boy, he was severely reprimanded for using such slang. The reprimand stung, but even back then, he loved words, especially those he thought unusual or exotic.

He found a pub just down the street from the corner where he had instructed Lottie to meet him. The name, "The Swot's Tot," appealed to Tom's love of rhyme as well as the pub itself providing some dark nooks where he and Lottie could sit together undisturbed. Tom waited impatiently at the corner of Holland Road and Russell Gardens. Lottie wasn't due for at least half an hour, and the chill in the air made Tom regret that he had chosen to forego an overcoat.

In the dark, he thought he glimpsed Lottie, walking swiftly toward him. Her head was down, her face slightly hidden under the gray wool cloche. She was clutching closed her matching knee-length wool overcoat, and her legs shimmered in dark-colored artificial silk stockings. Tom waved hesitantly, not yet sure that it was, indeed, Lottie, but the figure moving towards him was looking down as if carefully measuring her steps so she didn't see the wave.

Suddenly looking up and seeming to take a gulp of fresh air, Lottie saw Tom and smiled. She wiggled her fingers at him in a tentative greeting and mouthed, "Hello." She picked up her pace.

Tom raised his arm in a salute and grinned. He shifted from foot to foot, almost as if he were about to break into dance. Instead, he walked towards her, closing the distance between them more quickly. When he reached her, he moved toward an embrace but then stepped back. "So glad you came, Lottie," he said.

"Yes, Possum, I'm happy, too," Lottie answered almost breathlessly. It was the first time she noticed how much taller he was than she: her head didn't reach his shoulder. She felt small and, as a result, timid. Even standing on tiptoe, she would be unable to do as she instinctively wanted: to kiss his cheek.

"I've found a wonderful little pub where we can be warm and talk together without interruption," Tom said, steering her by the elbow south on Holland Road. "It's just down here," he said.

"Oh, Mr.—uh—Possum," Lottie corrected herself shyly, "I'm so glad we needn't stand out in the bad weather. I was hopin' you'd have somethin' planned." Lottie let herself be led by Tom's steering.

"Of course, dear girl, of course," Tom mumbled confidently. His initial nervousness had dissipated, replaced by a confidence that came naturally to him when dealing with those of a lower class. It wasn't snobbishness but a simple understanding that he was expected to take charge, be assertive, exercise control, and be *noblesse oblige.*

They settled at a small table in the back corner of the tavern. While Lottie was taking off her coat and folding it on the bench next to her, Tom ordered two whiskeys and two plates of pot roast with carrots and potatoes. "I haven't had supper, so I hope you'll eat as well to humor me."

Lottie didn't think it was a request so much as a strong suggestion. Although somewhat surprised that he hadn't asked her what *she* wanted, she was relieved that he took charge in this circumstance. "I ain't much of a drinker," she mumbled.

"If you'd like, I'll order you a beverage and drink both whiskeys, Lottie."

"Beer, then, please," Lottie responded.

Tom didn't like the smell of beer, especially on someone's breath, but he wanted Lottie to feel comfortable. He shrugged. "Whatever the lady chooses," he said.

Tom made sure that there was no awkward silence between them. Both during drinks and while consuming their meal, he kept up a steady stream of chatter, mostly about his life before England—his student days at Harvard, in Paris, and at Oxford because he couldn't stay in Germany when the war broke out.

When the dinner dishes were cleared away, and they'd ordered more drinks, Tom pulled some papers from his pocket. "I'd like your opinion on something I've written," Tom said. He unfolded the two sheets of paper and laid them on the table in front of Lottie. Immediately, a small round grease stain appeared in one corner where Lottie had spilled some juice from her roast.

"Oh, I've stained your paper," Lottie cried.

"No matter. It will be my remembrance of our first private meeting," Tom explained. "Shall I read to you or let you read on your own?"

Lottie looked blankly at the page in front of her. Did he mean, she wondered, that she was to read aloud, like reciting in front of a class? She shivered. "Perhaps it'd be better if you read to me," she said.

Tom did not pick up the pages. He clearly had memorized the words on the page. And because he left the page on the table, Lottie could read along as he recited the twelve lines. The page had only one correction: on the fourth line from the bottom, the word *And* deleted by typewriter strikeovers with the letter x. Otherwise, from the first words ("What are the roots. . . .") to the last (". . . a handful of dust") the page was clean and uncorrected.

Tom recited in a half-whisper because, he explained to Lottie, he didn't want to draw attention to them, but his voice still conveyed a building sense of desperation, of urgency, of a need that was spiritual but expressed almost carnally because of the images: stony rubbish, broken images, dead trees, red rock. Lottie found herself holding her breath through the recitation as if breathing might destroy the feeling.

"So," he concluded, now scooping up the pages, folding them, and pocketing them as if they were answers to a test he was about to administer to Lottie. "Tell me what you think."

"I ain't no poet, sir," she started. "Possum, I mean. I can only tell you how I feel. Would that be all right?"

"It's what I want," Tom answered. He had been sitting in a chair across the table from Lottie, but now he stood, slid down on the bench close to her, and put his arm around her shoulders. "Come in under my shadow," he chuckled, purposely altering the line from his poem.

"I feel kind of wobbly. Like somethin' terrible 'as

'appened an' there's no escapin' it. I feel frightened." Lottie snuggled closer to Tom.

"Afraid for yourself, Lottie?"

"For the world, Possum, for the whole world."

"Have I made you sad?" He looked down at the top of her head pressed against his chest. He rested his lips on her.

"Yes, but it's strange. It's like I was always sad, and you have just pointed that out to me, so now I see—"

"Now you see," Tom finished her sentence, "that your happiness has been an illusion all along."

"Yes, like a dream that I just awoke from."

Tom kissed the top of her head, then lifted her chin up toward his face. "I don't want you to cry, Lottie, just to see that the world's a sad and sorrowful place."

"I knew that already. You don't know what kind of life I've had," Lottie reproached him. She pulled away slightly.

Tom hugged her closer. "It doesn't matter, Lottie. What matters is that I've found you and treasure you." He ran his hand from her breast to her waist to her thigh. "I care for you."

Lottie did not answer immediately. His hand aroused her for a moment, but when he stopped, she wondered what was to happen next. Would he be bolder? Would she submit? Would they kiss? "Yes, I think you do," she finally said.

"And because I do, we will be correct. I'll find a way for us to be together, *really* together, in the future. For now, a sweet kiss will have to do." As Tom leaned down to kiss her, his intention was interrupted by the familiar pronouncement made in pubs all over England: "Hurry up, please, it's time." Tom laughed and released Lottie from his embrace. "It seems we are about to overstay our welcome." For a moment, he was relieved that the kiss was aborted because he did not want to taste the beer Lottie had drunk.

Lottie smiled and carefully arranged her cloche on her head.

"Let me put you in a carriage of some sort and send you home safely, Lottie," Tom said, standing up and heading to the bar to speak to the owner. When he returned to the table, he squeezed Lottie's hand, then raised it to his lips to kiss it. He detected a floral scent. "Your hand smells of hyacinth," he said with delight.

"Oh, no, Possum, 'tis lavender, I'm sure. Me soap." Lottie blushed.

"Ah, well, another time, dear, and perhaps earlier so we have more time together. The barman's arranged for your ride home, so wait here until it comes. I'll be in touch." Tom turned away, put on his cap, turned up the collar of his jacket around his neck, and walked out.

"Still a possum after all," Lottie said to herself.

8. Making Plans

The minute Tom got back to Clarence Gate Gardens, around midnight, he pulled the sheets of paper from his pocket and inserted one of them into his typewriter. Rolling the page to a blank line, he carefully typed:

Hurry up, please; it's time

Eleven p.m., The Swot's Tot

Holland Road & Richmond Gardens

Then pulled the paper from the typewriter and inserted it into a folder on the table. He felt that, somehow, those words carried more meaning than intended, but he'd have to see if that idea could work its way into this poem.

Tom put his hand on the folder as if he were seeking a heartbeat. This new poem, that he believed was both the most important and longest he would write, had been drifting around in his brain for months. He wrote lines in chunks, little narratives or snippets of ideas, which he had not yet connected in any logical way. He searched through his papers for lines that had no home in any poem or that he'd excised from a finished poem but saved because he liked the sound of them. He had chosen a line from Dickens' final novel, *Our Mutual Friend*, in which one of the characters refers to another who reads the newspaper to her dramatically, giving different voices to the characters of the stories. She says, "He do the Police in different voices," and that struck Tom as a perfect title for his poem—which, in his head, was a kind of compilation of different voices and different times throughout history, a time-machine newspaper, if you will. To the empty room, Tom said, "'e due tha poliss," and laughed at his attempt at Cockney. He repeated the line in American English, then in his halting command of the King's English, and finally in what he tried to accent like the Negro blues singers he'd heard on the streets of St. Louis. "Damnit," he muttered, unhappy with his recitation.

Opening the folder, he saw the small grease circle on the page. It turned his attention to what he was going to do about Lottie. How would he continue their rendezvous? Did he really want to? He idly wondered if he should let Vivien find out about Lottie 'by accident.' It would be his way of answering what he believed were her infidelities to him, a way of assuring her that he knew she was adulterous and he could be, too. But would he really consider having sex with Lottie?

Tom sighed loudly. He enjoyed the idea of sex, the talking about it, the descriptions of it among friends and in books, but engaging in it was problematic. His experience with Vivien was a source of consternation. In the short time they dated, she teased him with her attractiveness in many confusing ways. She'd look at him with desire in her eyes, lick her lips after saying something suggestive to him, and brush his cheek or arm with her fingers in a lingering way. It aroused him and often made him blush. He stammered. And, immediately, he felt ashamed, pulled at his chin in reproach, lowered his eyes, and moved away from her. Then Vivien would laugh. "It's just a silly game," she'd say and turn to speak about inane things like the weather or the color of the sky. More rarely, she would embrace him and, when she felt his erection against her, would pull back, look at him mischievously, and say, "Oh, Tom!" that was both reproach and invitation. Unable to endure this game and (truth be told) wishing to shed his troublesome virginity, he proposed.

By the end of the first week, Tom believed the marriage was a mistake. He had not satisfied Vivien nor himself. She had not satisfied or encouraged him. In fact, it was clear to Tom that the combination of his inexperience and her experience was a role reversal that neither could accept. Vivien wanted a man who could teach her something about physical relationships; Tom wanted a woman who was demure and innocent. She started calling him "Wonky-Penky", which she wouldn't explain but which he knew had to do with the fact that he sometimes could not complete their intercourse before he became impotent. They found themselves with exactly the opposite of what each desired. Yet, there was a bond: their failure was mutual, so they didn't blame each other but themselves and each took pity on the other for that failure and blame. Perhaps, Tom thought, they were meant to be together in some cruel plan of the universe: two sides of the same coin unable to be separated or, for that matter, merged. They were opposing parts of the same thing and could represent everything that was wrong with life today.

But what to do about Lottie? Was she to be another Virginia Woolf or Mary Hutchinson? Tom lit a cigarette and watched its smoke curling upward. He was attracted to women, and he knew that he could be attractive to them. He wasn't bad looking, he knew, despite his prominent aquiline nose and rather large ears. But he diminished these negative traits with generally handsome, stylish clothes, penetrating glances, a fleeting smile, and careful, slow speech that required others to listen to him in order to catch his meaning. Both Virginia and Mary, older than Vivien, thought they knew him, but he made sure to keep them off-balance, presenting to them a side of himself or of his opinions that were unexpected. Being generally 'mysterious' was his desire; it made him the centre of attention, a topic of conversation, without his having to do anything more than stand off to the side and let people wonder about him. Ezra had nicknamed him perfectly: Possum.

It was Lottie's class status that drew him to her. He knew he could easily impress her, but that wasn't his only purpose. He wanted to know more about her kind of person, what appealed to her, what repelled her, what puzzled her. She was his opportunity to explore and discover more about the "ordinary" folk of England. He suspected, and hoped to find evidence that they were, in fact, not very different from the tradespeople and serving classes of America whose simple honesty and forthrightness impressed him as so much more *real* than the attitudes and postures of the society to which he was born and in which he had been so carefully raised.

He thought that Lottie reminded him, perhaps just a bit, of Annie Dunne, his Irish-Catholic governess in St. Louis. He'd enjoyed his outings with Annie, who took him to church with her where the Catholic sense and sensibility—incense and shadows, lavish interiors and reverential silence—appealed to him the way his stern Unitarian upbringing did not. Annie's stern devotion to her religion fascinated and sometimes amused him as a child, for as much as she seemed enthusiastic to attend Mass, she also demonstrated a palpable fear of its strictures. But, even as a boy, he sensed an attractive incongruity of things and circumstances, and it became a motif in his life: to want what wasn't good for him and to be other than what was expected of him.

Tom noticed his cigarette almost burned down to his fingers, so he quickly stubbed it out in the ashtray. He squinted up at the "chandelier" (three bare bulbs attached to an iron strut) over the table, thinking he ought to turn it off so the bulbs wouldn't burn out. It was, his pocket watch told him, almost one a.m. He stood up, stretched, lit the oil lamp on the table and turned off the chandelier. "Tomorrow," he said aloud, replying to the question in his head: could he find a place where he could meet Lottie regularly? Then, taking the oil lamp with him, he decided to sleep in Vivien's bed (rather than in the lumpy one in the second bedroom) since Vivien would not return until tomorrow.

Lottie had managed to slip back into Hogarth House through the back door without disturbing anyone except Ned, whose turn it was to sit up and guard the doors.

"Oh, an' 'oo is there now?" he'd said, startled by Lottie's turning of the knob.

"It's just me, Lottie," she whispered quickly, not wanting to make a commotion.

"Where ha' ya been?" Ned rubbed his eyes. It was clear that he'd been sleeping.

"Out, so's you can see for yourself," Lottie answered impatiently. "Now get back to guardin', which you do so well I just might tell Mrs. Woolf about the quality of your work."

Lottie's veiled threat was not lost on Ned. "I ain't seen nothin' tonight," he assured her.

She was quick to find her way through the dark house to her room, to change into her nightclothes and to snuggle under the covers where she said her usual quick bedtime prayer for herself and her family. Looking up into the darkness, so dark she could not even see the ceiling above her, she sighed.

His brief caress and dispassionate kiss disappointed her,

and at the same time, she was relieved that nothing more had been proposed. Lottie fell asleep without effort because she had been exhausted by the encounter with the still-mysterious Possum.

The next morning, earlier than she wanted, but at the usual time of five a.m., she was helping cook breakfast for the Woolfs.

"You look knackered today, Lottie. Perk up, we've got rugs to beat later," Cook announced.

Lottie nodded weakly while she stirred the beans. "I'm fine." The reddish-brown sauce and beans bubbled noisily, so Lottie turned the heat down under them. "I'm a wee bit tired 'cause I was out last night for a bit o' supper an' a beer." Lottie noticed that the careful pronunciation that she'd been trying to develop had fallen away because of her fatigue; she'd slipped back into the more familiar and easier sounds she'd grown up with. She coughed.

"I saw you leave, dearie. Where'd you go that made you so tired?" The cook was slicing the bread, getting it ready to toast lightly on the stove.

"Up Holland Road a ways. I met someone at a pub for dinner and a drink or two. We talked for so long that it was late when I finally headed home."

"Goin' out durin' the week does no good for your working time, Lottie," Cook admonished.

"Yes, Cook, I know." Lottie barely managed to stifle a yawn while she pulled the pot of beans off the stove and onto the table. "The beans are ready," she announced.

"I'll just toast this bread. You prepare the tea, Lottie." Cook stood over the slices of bread, watching them closely so they wouldn't burn. "So, who was it you met that kept you out so late?"

Lottie looked into Cook's face, wondering if she were asking idly or if she were really curious to know. What does it matter? she thought. "You remember that gentleman, Mr. Eliot, the American?"

Cook's head turned quickly towards Lottie. "The married one who was here and touched you, then the next day brought you to the library on some excuse or other?"

"Don't be cross," Lottie answered. "He's really quite a gentleman."

Cook shook her head and turned back to the bread, using a fork to place the toasted slices on plates nearby. "Pour beans on them toasts and set the tea out as well. I'll take the one plate to the Missus; you take t'other to Mr. Leonard." Cook knew that Mr. Leonard would not notice Lottie's fatigue whereas Mrs. Woolf would and probably ask about it; it better to keep Lottie out of the Missus's sight. She fussed with the placement of the bread on the plates before she'd let Lottie add the beans. "Ain't much of a gentleman when he's a married man takin' you to dinner and drinks at a pub, I says."

Lottie picked up one of the trays. "Really, Cook, we just talked about—of all things—his poetry. He wanted my opinion."

As Lottie headed out of the kitchen balancing the tray carefully, she heard Cook call after her, "And what's the opinion of a kitchen maid mean t' anyone at all?" followed by a loud snort.

9. Other Matters

Although they'd managed to get a decent number of winter outfits by mid-December, Vivien's wardrobe went largely unused because of her chronic illnesses that rendered her bedridden for days or weeks at a time. She was in bed much of the day, being tended to by the housekeeper Ellen because Tom was at the bank, and at night when he got home and Ellen had departed, she complained of fatigue, often falling asleep while he sat at her bedside telling her about his day. Although he wouldn't say so, Tom was annoyed that she'd spent so much money on outfits that it seemed she would never wear; he hoped that, despite her illnesses that caused her weight to fluctuate wildly, she'd be able to use the clothes come Spring when his mother was due to arrive for a two-months holiday.

Meanwhile, he was free to visit with friends, usually on the weekend, who were not shy to reveal their relief that Vivien was not with him (although they politely expressed it with insincere regards for her well-being), and they gladly wined and dined him without reserve. He was, after all, interesting company for them, not only because he was American but also because they never quite knew if he were going to be outgoing and gregarious or sullen and sarcastic; either way, they found him entertaining. Depending on whoever was hosting him – old American friends from college or new British friends in literary circles – Tom acted the part he thought most appropriate to the occasion: learned scholar, sardonic critic, or innocent foreigner. Yet, as much as he enjoyed playing these roles, he'd arrive back home exhausted and irritated, feeling he could never just be himself. He'd sit at his typewriter, both angry and alarmed, and he seemed to be losing any sense of who he truly was. His personality, he felt, was dissolving into thin air.

Intellectually, Tom knew that Vivien was not to blame for his nervousness, but emotionally, he found it easy to accuse her as the source of it. "You know I can't work properly either at the bank or on my writing when you're ill like this."

"I can't help it," Vivien would whine, the pitch of her voice rising to a level that made Tom shiver.

"You know there's nothing more I can do for you, Viv. You must set your mind to getting healthier by yourself." As usual, when they had a row, he would retreat to the doorway of the bedroom, ready to quit that threshold when he felt the situation hopeless. He was tightly gripping the lintel.

"By myself?" Vivien asked bitterly. "While I am here sick all day, you are working. When I am here sick on the weekend, you are gallivanting from one gathering to the next from noon until after bedtime. I'm by myself all the time, Tom, like an old wodge. Do you see me getting better by myself?"

"I think that you don't even understand what it means to be by yourself, Viv. You rely on people to care for you. First, it was your parents and even your brother; now, it's me and Ellen, and even your friend Lucy Thayer, who is too sympathetic. Perhaps if you were left alone, truly alone, you'd find the strength to pick yourself up out of these mad illnesses." Tom felt a throbbing in his left eye, the sign that his hands would soon start to tremble, his voice to crack, and his need to flee be overwhelming.

"You're mean and nasty, Tom." Vivien dropped her head to her chin in surrender. She could never win an argument with him.

"I'm sorry, Viv," he said softly after taking a deep breath, "because I don't mean to hurt you. I don't know what comes over me." He had been taught self-reliance, but he had also been taught to always be courteous and polite, to avoid arguing because it was vulgar, so these times with Vivien made him churn with self-loathing.

"Tom, I'll try what you say, that is, to improve my attitude about myself. I think, however, that we need to decide what to do to make *you* better. You're wound up too tight."

Tom sighed. His fingers ached from gripping the doorway. He loosened his hand, opening it from a fist and stretching his fingers outward. "What shall we do?"

Vivien brightened. She always felt better when Tom asked her advice. "First, you need a place to write. Perhaps a small room somewhere? You know, a kind of secret hideaway of your very own."

Tom realized that Vivien's suggestion was a true solution. He'd have a place to write without her constant interruptions for medicine, food, or affection while she was bedridden. And, he smiled. It would mean a place where he could bring Lottie. "What a splendid suggestion, Vivien, although I'm not sure we can afford it."

"We've managed quite well. As long as we're prudent, love, I'm sure we'll manage." Vivien clapped with delight. "So, Penky, get on it, eh?"

Tom laughed. "I shall. But you must promise to think only positive thoughts about yourself."

Vivien nodded, then added suddenly, "Oh, a letter has come for you from Ezra in Italy." She pulled the envelope from under her pillow. "I almost forgot to give it you. But, here," she offered, holding it out to Tom.

He looked at the envelope with a grin. He really enjoyed his correspondence with Ezra Pound, who had encouraged him to write from the very first time that he'd read Eliot's poetry, which was shown to him by Tom's friend, Conrad Aiken. After carefully opening the missive, he read with growing delight that Ezra was going to Paris the week before Christmas and was inviting Tom to meet him there for a brief holiday. "Look, Viv, he has invited me to meet him in Paris next week."

Vivien smiled bravely. She understood that it meant Tom going alone; she was clearly not invited, which disappointed her. However, now that they'd settled their dispute, she had no wish to argue again. "That's wonderful, Tom. Do go. It will be my perfect opportunity to demonstrate my new attitude about regaining my health."

"Yes, I think I shall, Viv. I'll write Ezra this very night. I promise it won't cost much, and the bank owes me some holiday time anyway. I'll look for a small hideaway when I return. Oh, this is just what I need!" Tom moved into the bedroom from the doorway and knelt on the bed to lean in toward his wife. "A kiss for good fortune?" he asked sweetly.

Knowing that her husband wanted nothing more than that kiss, Vivien offered her cheek to him. She was disappointed but resigned to what seemed always to be the inevitable conclusion of their spats: neutral ground, calm and decidedly polite affection.

Tom managed his week in Paris, spending the final three days with Ezra and his wife, Dorothy. For the first part of the week, he spent time in a small hotel where he wrote all day. His room overlooked the busy Boulevard Saint-Germain, and despite the cold, he kept his balcony doors ajar so he could hear and see the bustle of people three stories below.

Waking at seven, Tom would quickly dress and go to the nearest café for coffee and a croissant or baguette, glance through the newspaper, then return to his room to write until one, at which time he'd go for lunch and a long walk, often to the Luxembourg Gardens, before returning to his room to freshen up for dinner. Working on the long poem that he wanted to show to Ezra, he found himself wishing he had some of his books with him to check his allusions and references. During his walks, he'd sometimes hear a snatch of a stray conversation that strangely reminded him of London. One day, walking near the Seine, he saw a swirling oil slick in the water, moving with the current and dotted with refuse—a discarded wrapper, a balled-up envelope, an orange peel—and he was reminded of the polluted Thames back near St. Mary Magdelene Church in Woolwich where he sometimes strolled at lunch.

He went back to his room that day and outlined a section of the poem that described the Thames and told of an unfortunate encounter between a young girl and a callous young man. He thought of Lottie, wondering if she'd had a boyfriend. Next to his notes, he wrote her name with a question mark after it. Then, feeling a little guilty, the next day, he sent a telegram to Vivien: "Missing you, darling. As ever, Tom." He also found an original Raoul Dufy for her that he thought might please her and lift her spirits because of its bright colors.

His meetings with Ezra were both enjoyable and fruitful. More often than not, Dorothy Pound would excuse herself to leave them alone to talk. When she was present, they spoke mostly of social or personal matters but never about poetry.

"How is dear Vivien, Tom?" she'd ask sincerely.

"Still a bit under the weather, but surely sorry that she couldn't come along," Tom would answer. It was his stock reply whenever anyone inquired after Vivien.

"Well, I hope our encouragement to you two will not come to naught," Ezra said.

Tom shook his head. "Ezra, it was your advice and encouragement that decided me to marry Vivien, thereby sealing my commitment to staying in London. I'm glad to be done with the pretense of becoming an American philosophy professor."

Ezra laughed. "Your talent, my friend, shall not be wasted on the *illiterate* of America, not if I have anything to say about it. And your wife is quite the catch, too." He patted Tom's knee with approval.

Tom looked first at Dorothy. "Please don't take offense at what I'm about to say," he began. "Vivien and I are not suited to one another, I'm afraid."

Dorothy didn't gasp, but she leaned back and away from Tom as if his words physically stung her. Ezra quickly commented, "You're not thinking clearly, Possum."

Eliot laughed. "Well, Rabbit, then you'll need to set me straight, I'll guess." It was Ezra who had christened Tom as "Possum" and, in return, Tom got to calling Ezra "Rabbit," after the Joel Chandler Harris character, a wily and clever hero in that allegorical world of animals. Sometimes, when they spoke in private, they adopted the dialect of the Harris tales.

"I'll say this once, Possum, then shut the hell up. Were it not for your relationship with Vivien, whatever the nature of it may be or has become, it's because she's in your life that you write your poetry. You owe her some goodwill, if not also gratitude, for that."

Tom looked at Ezra for a long moment before he said quietly, "I'll remember that, Rabbit. Thank you."

On their last day together in Paris, Tom and Ezra walked along the Seine to the Parvis Notre Dame, the wide plaza in front of the cathedral. "Should I continue?" Tom asked, referring to the twenty pages of the poem he had shown to Ezra two days before.

"It's clearly not finished, and what's there needs a great deal more thought and editing," Ezra answered, "but yes, of course, keep working. I think you're onto something."

"Vivien left a message for me at the hotel last night. Our phone is installed. However, the thought of returning to London, to the bank, to Vivien, to that completely mad scene with the Bloomsbury Set makes me sick to my stomach."

"Good," Ezra answered. "That's exactly what needs to be expressed in this poem that you're writing. The world is almost in tatters, and you must be the one to record its demise."

"Ezra, I'm afraid—"

Pound interrupted his friend. "Whatever happens to you, Tom, it is for the good of the poem. You'll see that, trust me, and I hope you'll use that knowledge wisely."

Early 1921

10. Back To Reality

Paris had refreshed him. He was also buoyed by the fact that their telephone service had been restored, and when he arrived home from work at their flat one late January afternoon, Vivien seemed completely cured. She fussed over him, even insisting on removing his shoes and massaging his feet.

"Really, Viv, although that's quite nice, I wish you'd stop." He was embarrassed by the intimacy of her rubbing his stockinged feet.

"Tom, just sit back and enjoy it. If you just relax, you might find it quite soothing."

Actually, Tom felt it to be exactly the opposite, that is, sexually exciting, and he became more disturbed. To stop Vivien from touching him, he said, "I'm so glad we've the phone again. I think I'll give a call to Virginia, and perhaps she and Leonard can receive us sometime for lunch." He walked across the room to the small telephone table and sat in the single chair beside it.

"Hello, Virginia!" he said loudly. "We were hoping to see you and Leonard."

Vivien shrugged her shoulders, surrendering to Tom's wish to be left alone. She pointed to his bedroom, then herself, indicating she was leaving the room while he spoke on the phone. Tom nodded.

Into the phone, he said, "Yes, of course, that sounds delightful." He smiled. Then, after listening to a moment, his smile faded, and he knitted his brow. "Oh, I see," he said, "yes, of course I'll tell her. Thank you." Tom covered the phone's speaker for a moment and sighed loudly. Then: "Well, I must run. Vivien needs me. We'll see you then, thanks." He hung up, replacing the phone on the table.

Vivien returned from the bedroom. "You really are awful at caring for your things, Tom. All your clothes are balled up. It will take Ellen hours to launder and iron out those wrinkles." Then, laughing lightly, she added, "You're the same in the kitchen. You can cook decently, but you leave the room in shambles."

Ignoring her remark, Tom said quietly. "We've been invited to lunch at the Woolfs next week. Mary Hutchinson will be there, but without John, of course. She'll be with Clive instead."

"I think it's scandalous how those people flaunt their infidelities. It makes me uncomfortable." Vivien fluffed the ruffles on her blouse.

"Oh?" Tom asked. "More than what you do, Viv?" He sneered.

Vivien looked up. "What do you mean, Tom?" She was surprised by his change in tone.

In trying to develop his English accent, Tom spoke deliberately and slowly. Now, irritation and choler were added, so his words seemed to ooze out of his mouth. "Virginia told me to tell you that they'd posted a copy of my book, *Poems*, as you requested, to Mr. Charles Buckle. They asked me if I wanted him put on the recipient list for announcements."

"Oh, Tom, don't be upset. I wanted Charles to know how successful you are."

"Really?" When they'd first met, Vivien had said she'd ended an engagement with someone. After they'd been married, her brother Maurice told him that she'd been engaged to a schoolteacher named Charles Buckle, but the fellow broke it off and was drafted after Viv's mother objected strenuously. The family suspected that Vivien and Mr. Buckle had been— scandalously—intimate and pronounced Charles Buckle, a scoundrel whom they would not allow their daughter to marry. Tom was clearly the rebound choice. "I didn't know you were still in touch with him." Tom moved to the bookcase against the wall and squatted down in front of it.

"Tom, please. You were in Paris with your 'Rabbit.' Two grown men calling each other stupid names like 'Possum' and 'Rabbit.' I was home alone and sick. To cheer myself up, I thought I'd let Charles Buckle know that I didn't need him, that

I'd married better—a successful poet." Vivien started by protesting but ended up whining.

Tom pulled a thin book from the bookcase. "You should have sent him *this*," he said angrily. He threw the book toward Vivien, and it landed with a thud on the floor. The slim blue-cloth book had white-silver lettering; it was *Down The Silver Stream of the Thames*, a brief study of the topography of the Thames. "We've talked of this before, Viv. The title alludes to the Prothalamion of Edmund Spenser, a wedding poem. And you've inscribed it, 'For Charles, with love from Vivie.' Why didn't you return *this* to him instead of sending him *my* book?"

"I told you. You left me alone and took off for Paris. I didn't think it would upset you."

"And did you tell Virginia and Leonard to inscribe my book to him as well? In fact, why have you kept his address? When will you invite him to tea? To dancing?" Tom's voice gained volume and anger as he spoke.

Vivien shrunk in place, putting her head down. "Tom, please. Let's talk quietly. I'll make some tea, and we'll have some biscuits and talk." She retreated to the kitchen.

Tom picked up the book from the floor and replaced it in the bookcase. He sat down heavily, no longer feeling refreshed from his Parisian sojourn. He felt the room was too hot, too close.

Vivien came in with a tray of tea and biscuits and sat next to him on the divan, balancing the tray on her lap. "We'll both feel better after we talk and see that what I did was just harmless, nothing to be upset about." She smiled tentatively.

Tom folded his arms. He didn't want tea or biscuits. He didn't want to talk to Vivien. He watched her pouring tea into cups, adding some sugar. After placing a plate of biscuits between them on the divan, she put the tray on the floor at her feet and picked up a cup and saucer, offering them to Tom.

He shook his head and leaned back, staring across the room to avoid looking at Vivien's face. He folded his arms across his chest to hide the angry trembling in his hands.

She kept the cup of tea for herself, taking a small sip of the steaming liquid. Then, she said quietly, "Tom, forgive me, please. I meant nothing by it."

Tom wanted to ask her if she'd meant nothing by spending almost more time with Bertie Russell than with him during the first year of their marriage if she meant nothing by going out nights with her friend Lucy to dance halls and coming home to tell Tom about some "marvelous dancers" she'd met if she meant nothing by flirting with other men either in person or in writing them vaguely suggestive letters. Tom knew about it all.

When he didn't say anything, Vivien added, "Sometimes, Tom, I think you're actually glad that I talk to other men, as if you're happy I'm not bothering you."

"Don't be stupid, Vivien," he snapped, but the blush that rose in his cheeks contradicted his denial.

"You can be so cold, Tom."

"And you, shamefully, can be exactly the opposite. You embarrass me, Vivien."

"When we first met, you called me vivacious."

Tom snorted. "But as a married woman, you have a certain responsibility to act more properly."

"As if you knew anything about how women should or shouldn't act," Vivien challenged.

"By sending a copy of my book to Charles Buckle," Tom said, bringing the argument back to its original point, "you have embarrassed yourself and disappointed me. In fact, I wouldn't be surprised if Mr. Buckle were not asking himself right now what kind of fool I am to have taken you as a wife?" He looked at Vivien then, with cruelty in his eyes. "I shouldn't have married you, Vivien. I should have just left a 5£ note on the nightstand for you."

Vivien went pale.

"I need fresh air," Tom said, retrieving his shoes and tying the laces. "The matter is closed, Viv." He reached into his pocket but then thought better of dropping some money on the tea tray; he had been cruel enough.

At the door, he put on his overcoat and hat. Before closing the door, he tipped his hat to Vivien. "Good afternoon, dear." He decided to head to the kitchen door of Hogarth House.

Once outside, however, Tom had second thoughts about going to the Woolfs' residence, even if just to the back door. What if Virginia or Leonard discovered him there? They'd believe him a proper fool.

Instead, he decided to go to Regents' Park, a short walk from his apartment. Already cold, it would soon be dark, so he hurried along the street, hoping to have some time to cool off in the park before it got too dark. He needed to think clearly. When he reached the intersection, he saw a pub out of the corner of his eye. That was surely a better destination than the park, he thought, turning abruptly to his left.

He'd never been in this particular establishment, but it seemed decent enough. On entering, he removed his hat and looked around: only a few patrons at the bar and two middle-aged women at a table. He nodded to the barman and took a dark table in a corner near the back, placing his hat and coat on the empty chair. He cleared his throat and said loudly, "A scotch, please."

After his drink was served, Tom leaned back in his chair, trying to ease the tension out of his shoulders. He closed his eyes and shook his head as if scolding himself. The joy of seeing Ezra and being in Paris was completely gone, replaced by an angry regret. He was sorry to have lost his temper, sorry to have made so much of Vivien's thoughtlessness. Yet, he wondered if he were not even sorrier for himself, burdened with a wife for whom he always seemed to be making excuses, with a job that everyone thought beneath him, with poetry that too few appreciated, and with a family whose expectations of him he could not possibly meet. He rubbed his forehead with anxiety.

"But I ain't never really loved 'im," a woman's voice said, carrying easily through the almost empty room.

"Then what'd you marry him for, innit?" A second voice asked, even louder.

The barman said, "Keep it quiet an' to yerselves," with some annoyance.

"Yeah, all right. All right," the first lady answered, then said something in a hoarse whisper to her companion.

The second woman laughed, more of a cackle, then said, "We've got t' be ladies, 'aven't we now?" But, despite their protestation, they continued their conversation at a low enough volume that no one could hear them.

Tom drank his whiskey quickly, put his hat and coat back on, and put 2£ on the bar to settle his bill. When he stepped outside, intending to head home, he whispered to himself, "Then what'd you marry her for, innit?" He would kiss Viv when he got home and accept her apology. It would not, he knew, dispel his feelings of despair and hopelessness.

11. Barely Possum

It had started as a mere tic in the corner of his left eye, pulsing beneath the skin that sent him rushing to a mirror to see how bad it was. No, hardly perceptible to others, Tom realized, but inside, it felt like the beating of a rather large drum. After a few moments, if he sat very still and consciously breathed in and out, it went away. Perhaps, he thought, he just needed glasses. He finished dressing and went out to find a hackney. He'd be late for lunch at the Woolfs, as he intended, so everyone might fuss over him.

The week before, Tom had ensconced Vivien in a nursing home, one of her recurring illnesses so bad that she needed twenty-four-hour attention. Assuring her that he'd visit each day, he tried to balance his bank work with his evening round of critical reviews, sitting with Vivien for an hour or two and preparing for his family's arrival in two months. Any invitation to a meal was welcomed because he'd dismissed their maid, Ellen, for two months. He told her that, with Vivien in the nursing home, he temporarily had no need for her services; in reality, he could not afford to pay her and meet the expenses of Vivien's nursing home stay.

"I'm sorry, Lottie, things have not turned out as I wanted," he whispered to the young maid who was taking his coat and hat.

"No matter," Lottie whispered back and disappeared into an anteroom.

Tom almost called after her but saw Virginia coming towards him. He smiled effusively. "So nice to see you."

Virginia touched her cheek to his in greeting and grasped his hands. She immediately noticed how cold his skin was; she thought it was not from the February weather but internal, as if there were ice rather than fire fueling his existence. When she stepped back and looked at him, she noticed that he was particularly pale. "Tom, are you all right?"

He laughed out loud. "And why wouldn't I be? Stop mother-henning me, Virginia!" He felt his hand start to tremble, so he shoved it in his pocket. "I'm sorry that Vivien—" he started his usual excuse.

Virginia interrupted him as she looped her arm in his, leading him to the parlor. "No regrets, Tom, no regrets."

For a moment, as they walked from the hall, Tom imagined that Virginia's arm pressed against his suggested an overture to sexuality, but then he shook his head in denial and disbelief; how could he be so vain?

They had a pleasant but unusually subdued afternoon because Tom seemed distracted much of the time, answering inquiries with only a word or two, commenting hardly at all, and sitting silently with his head down as if deep in thought when the others fell to gossiping. He excused himself early but whispered to Lottie as she was helping him into his coat, "Meet me at the corner for a moment."

Lottie had carelessly thrown her coat over her dress and apron so she could meet with Tom quickly. When she reached him on the corner, she was shocked at how frail he seemed, although she let him pull her close to him, grasping both her hands in his. "I've run into a bit of a jam, Lottie. My wife is very ill in a nursing home. My work is rather busy. My mother, sister, and brother are arriving in a few months for an extended visit. I don't think we shall meet again for some time, perhaps September or October."

Lottie stiffened. "There's no need to make excuses or lie, Possum, if you're no longer interested in me. I've a life of my own, y'know."

"You can't know how that hurts me, Lottie," Tom answered, squeezing her hands even tighter. "I want us to be together."

"I need to think this through, you understand. This ain't an ordinary courting, what with you being married and all."

"Yet you need to know, Lottie, that my marriage was nothing more than a rebound, you understand?"

She shook her head and pulled her hands away from him.

"It means that I only married Vivien because a girl in America refused me." Why, he thought to himself, would Emily Hale suddenly pop into his mind? He'd met her in 1912 when he was at Harvard and thought himself vaguely in love with her. When he left America two years later to study in Paris, he'd written to her, indicating his interest in her. She'd rebuffed him. By the end of the following year, he'd married Vivien. "So, now that I've met you, I am regretting this marriage every day."

Lottie looked at him with disappointment. "And how long have you been married?"

"Not quite six years, Lottie," he answered, "and I'm so very tired of it all." He cupped her face in his hands.

She felt the chill in his fingers spread through her cheeks. Her teeth almost ached from the cold. "You're so cold," she remarked, wanting somehow to warm him but not knowing how.

"Please, Lottie, tell me you'll give me time to figure this all out." He leaned down, drawing his face closer to hers as if for a kiss.

She saw a tiny throbbing at the corner of his left eye and felt the cold coming off him like a wind out of nowhere. She was frightened but also concerned for him. She wasn't sure she could help him, but she said, "I ain't goin' nowhere, 'sfar as I know. I'll still be a housemaid in a few months, I'll wager."

Then, he kissed her, not innocently or sheepishly as he'd done before, but aggressively and insistently, as if demanding what she owed him. "And so I've sealed our fates together," he said with authority. "I'll come to you when I can." He turned away without another word.

His bravado with Lottie lasted only as far as getting inside the door at Clarence Gate Gardens. There, in the silent dark of the empty apartment, he sat at the dining table and wept. It did not help him to remember what Ezra had said: "Whatever happens to you, Tom, it is for the good of the poem."

His family arrived on schedule in the second week of June announcing that they were staying for two months. Vivien, who'd been released from the nursing home, made excuses to decamp from London and stay "in the country." Tom understood and made excuses to his family, allowing that Vivien would see them only occasionally during their visit. Tom gave up his apartment to his mother and sister, installed his elder brother, Henry, in a place owned by friends and, himself moved to temporary quarters. He entertained them as best he could, in particular introducing his mother to some of the aristocracy who sponsored many of London's artists and writers. Still, only his sister, Charlotte, expressed some pleasure in having met and talked with Vivien. It was clear to Eliot that his family would never truly approve of his marriage, his wife, or his life choice.

A few days before their planned departure for home, Henry suggested that Tom accompany him on a second visit to the British Museum; he wanted, particularly, to "inspect more closely the Elgin Marbles."

As they made their way through the various rooms of the museum, Tom said, "You know, Henry, I have tried to please Mother as best I could."

Henry nodded, then seeing that they'd finally entered the huge, cavernous room holding the fragments of the Marbles attached firmly to the walls, he sat down, inviting Tom to join him. "Mother would only be completely pleased if you had followed her plan for you: remain in America, teach philosophy at Harvard, and marry an agreeable American girl, preferably one from a good New England family."

"I would have done so had the first girl I loved accepted me." Tom was recalling his conversation with Lottie.

"I'm not so sure, Tom. She was an actress, I understand." Henry had said the word 'actress' with clear disdain.

"Am I never to please them?" Tom was referring not only to his mother but to his deceased father as well.

"Just as much as they have never pleased you, Tom. You would never really do what they wanted once you were old enough to make your own way."

"But I am *still* dependent on them, on you, to some extent. I cannot support my life with a wife on my own, it seems."

Henry patted his knee. "Father thought that arranging a trust for you, rather than outright cash, would help you see your choices more clearly." He hesitated, then plunged ahead: "And when you have children? It will be worse then, Tom."

Tom shook his head. "There will be no children in my future."

Henry looked at him a moment. "It's not my business to pry, Tom, so I will only say that I hope you find happiness somehow. You will not find it with Vivien, I'm afraid."

"You don't approve, I see. Yet, I must tell you, Henry, without her, I would not be a poet. Something about her, something about *us*—she and I together—is the root of my creative endeavors."

"She inspires you?" Henry asked incredulously. He had sensed, even seen, the distance between them, as if they were strangers thrown together, not a married couple.

"No, I don't think so. It's something other than that. She recognizes the poet in me, draws him out, and encourages him. She's really an undeniable part of my poetic process, like my doorway to writing."

Henry shook his head. "I'm nothing more than a businessman, after all, so I don't think I'll ever understand you or your poetry. I only know this, Tom, sometimes when I read what you've written (even some of your letters), I think I can *feel* what you're saying, though I'd be hard-pressed to explain it to someone else. Mother's right about this: you have a gift. I will do what I can to encourage its continued development."

Tom patted his brother's back. "Thank you, Henry, from the bottom of my heart."

When the Eliots sailed for America, Tom was relieved to get back into his own apartment and to welcome Vivien there although he kept the small temporary place, telling Viv it would be his "writing retreat." Then, within two weeks of his family's departure, Tom's tics and chills returned, this time accompanied by nightly sweats and headaches. He refused Vivien's ministrations, fearing that in trying to take care of him, she would herself fall back into illness. The only bright spot in his life was to find that Henry had secretly taken Tom's old typewriter and replaced it with a newer one.

Tom insisted he couldn't fall ill. He had his job at the bank, his reviews and critical essays to write, and his long poem that was still, he believed, more complete inside his head than on the page. Then there was Lottie, to whom he had promised he would somehow return.

One weekend in August, beastly hot, Tom was working at the table, writing his monthly piece for *The Dial*, an American publication owned by his Harvard classmate Scofield Thayer. Suddenly, his hands froze. "Viv! Please come help!" he called; she was reading in the parlor.

"What's wrong, Tom?" she asked, walking casually into the dining room. She looked down to see his hands still and frozen, hovering over the typewriter keys. "What's wrong with your hands?"

"I—I don't know. I'm paralyzed." He kept staring helplessly at his hands.

Vivien pulled a chair closer to him. She began to massage his temples gently. "There. You must relax. Close your eyes now."

Within a moment, his hands dropped onto the typewriter keys. Tom raised them, turned them palm inward, and stared at them. "What's happening to me?"

"Vivien put her arms around his neck. "I insist, Tom, that we take you to a nerve specialist as soon as possible. No resisting. No refusing. I insist."

He dropped his hands into his lap. There was a thin line of sweat above his upper lip. "I am so afraid, Viv."

"I know, Tom," she answered soothingly. She smiled, but she, too, was afraid.

The specialist's recommendation was that Tom takes himself out of London "indefinitely" to effect a complete recovery; Vivien agreed, but Tom did not. The result was that he and Vivien had a blazing row on their return to the apartment, complete with shouting and throwing objects at walls. When Tom snapped angrily at their dog, Dinah, who had thought the yelling great fun and joined in by yapping loudly, Vivien scooped up the little dog in her arms protectively and sneered. "Then off to your bloody hell of a writing retreat where you can rot for all I care."

Tom was glad to leave, and the brisk September afternoon wind cooled him down as he made his way to the third-floor bedsitter he was renting on Seymour Street, not far from where he and Vivien had lived before they'd moved to their current residence. It wasn't much of a place, but he stocked it with pencils, pens, and paper to do his writing in relative peace. The furnished room had a compact cooking stove (that doubled as an extra heater in winter), a small credenza, a single bed, a rickety table and two chairs. On the credenza was a basin which, if needed for washing, could be filled with water from the bathroom down the hall. There were hooks on the back of the door to hang clothes. Tom sat down without removing his overcoat. He sat down and scribbled a hasty note to Lottie, folded it into an envelope along with a 5£ note, and sealed it.

Once Tom had given the note to a bike messenger to deliver to Lottie at Hogarth House (almost ten miles away), he returned to the room with some tea and biscuits from the local tea shop, two plates of bangers and mash from the cookshop, and a bottle of whiskey. He put everything except the whiskey on the stove to keep warm and hung up his overcoat, hat, and suit jacket. He was confident that he only need to wait for Lottie to appear; he felt certain she would not refuse him.

Three hours later, the food drying out on the radiator and the whiskey bottle almost half-empty, Lottie knocked at the door. Tom didn't just let her in. He pulled her into his arms, then sat her on the bed. "I knew you'd come, dear Lottie."

He knew he could've had his way with her. That knowledge gave him enough confidence to resist taking her sexually, especially after she confessed that she was a virgin. He had no wish to ruin the poor girl; he wanted only to feel that he *could*.

He did not ask her, nor would he let her touch him at all. Instead, he kissed her, touched her everywhere, unbuttoning her clothes so his hands could feel her hot flesh, and then hugged her protectively. "Don't worry, Lottie. I'm not a scoundrel after all."

He sat with her at the table, and they ate the now soggy meals. They took turns taking swigs of whiskey from the bottle and drank their tea holding hands. They laughed, Tom, feeling especially good about these moments of unguarded carelessness. He teased Lottie about her accent as well as demonstrating his own imitations of British English. He sang music hall songs for her and taught her to dance the Cubana Glide while he hummed the melody.

As it got dark, Tom's mood became more somber. "I have to go away for a while, Lottie," he said finally. "I'm quite sick, and the doctor has recommended I leave London for a time."

"How long?" Lottie asked, disappointed.

"Months, I'm sure," Tom said. "It is the thought of you that's kept me sane so far, but now that we've been intimate, I don't want to hurt you. If I see you again before I am cured, I shall take advantage of you, which I don't want to do."

She had enjoyed his caresses but was too timid to say so. "But what's wrong with you?"

"*Aboulie* in French. To put it plainly, Lottie, I don't give a damn about anything."

"But you care for me, surely?"

"I do, but you must see how that is easily affected by my illness. If I truly cared for you as I thought I initially did, I would not have invited you here, not have molested you as I did. It is only my last shred of morality that keeps me from ravishing you completely. I must go away. I'm a danger to you now."

Lottie realized that she had reached the limit of her

understanding of Tom, this mysterious stranger who fascinated her so. What was he talking about? Why must he leave? She saw in his eyes a kind of panic, of fear, which she did not understand. "As you require, sir." Putting that formal distance between them with the simple word, *sir*, helped her to pretend indifference.

They said little after that, and they helped each other tidy up the room and dress to depart. On the street, Tom called a cab for her, gave the driver her address and the fare, and hugged Lottie briefly. "When I'm better," he promised, sending her off into the night. He decided to sleep in the bedsitter tonight, in the bed where the scent of Lottie's lavender would lull him to sleep.

12. Margate

Of course, Vivien was relieved to see Tom when he returned from his overnight stay at the bedsitter; however, she again suggested following the specialist's advice—to leave London for a better environment—after she noticed that Tom could barely control his shaking and trembling, even having difficulty lifting a teacup or knotting his tie. "Tom, please!" Vivien begged, her concern evident in her voice.

After almost six years of marriage, Tom knew that Vivien's worries about him would end in only one way: she would help him convalesce and then fall ill herself, and he would have to take care of her. It was not a situation he enjoyed. "Vivien, I'm telling you that I simply cannot leave my position at the Bank. On the other hand, they might allow me a month's leave."

"You need at least that, I fear," she said.

"We'll see. I thought a holiday in Margate might do the trick, perhaps a month if you are willing to accompany me." This is what he'd been planning: getting away but not too far, keeping Vivien with him and away from her temptations to wander, spending time together so they might restart their relationship, and the bonus being that he might make Vivien over into a "better" person. He was tired of making excuses for her to family and friends.

"But the doctor said you needed to do this rest cure alone, darling," Vivien protested.

Tom couldn't tell if she was sincere or merely being polite. "You don't want to accompany me?" A twitch was starting to develop in his left eye.

"Of course I do! I just don't want to be contrary to the specialist's orders." Vivien hesitated to embrace him; he seemed so fragile to her.

"Margate will do you some good, too, Viv, I'm certain." He smiled sweetly.

"All right, then. We shall go to Margate and be cured of

all our ills," Vivien agreed, sighing. She actually thought Margate a bit shabby, but it was better than staying in London. Perhaps she could convince Tom to move on from Margate once his recuperation were underway.

In the succeeding two weeks, all arrangements had been finalized. Dinah, the dog, was boarded with Vivien's brother. A stray cat that had adopted them was given to a friend. The bank had generously given Tom three months' leave, as per the specialist's prescription, with a regimen of being isolated and alone and of reading "for pleasure only" for two hours a day, so Tom had to write to colleagues to postpone all of his commitments until January 1922. And, when the month in Margate would be done, he was invited to stay in southern France at a villa belonging to a potential patron, Lady Rothmere.

On October fifteenth, the Eliots arrived at the Albemarle Hotel in Margate. It was not the most modern of accommodations, but Mr. Beazley, the proprietor, was extremely solicitous. At first, Tom was tense, wondering what he was going to do with himself all day without his review work; Vivien went out and came back the second day with a mandolin. It was more a toy than a serious instrument, but the music store provided her with a printed page of the notes of the G-major scale. "The chap said that he has tuned the mandolin, so you need only follow this paper to practice the scale."

Tom was skeptical, but once he tried plucking the strings, he smiled. It fascinated him that he could actually make the instrument sound like something other than noise. He decided he would practice daily; besides, he couldn't smoke when he played, needing both hands for the instrument, so he was starting to feel better already.

Vivien wrote letters for Tom during their stay to keep him from exerting himself too much. She noticed that, in less than two weeks, he already seemed less frail and more composed, even allowing her one night to lay her head in his lap. "I'm glad we are here, Tom."

"Yes, Viv, it is the start of what I've needed for too long."

He absently stroked her hair and hummed quietly.

"What is that tune?"

He repeated the tune softly, then said, "Vivien, get up a moment. Let me show you." He retrieved the mandolin and carefully plucked the strings, reproducing on the mandolin the tune he'd been humming. He smiled at Viv. Again, he played the nineteen notes on the mandolin, but this time followed closely by a new set of ten notes and his singing: "Ah hate to see," pausing and closing his eyes, "the ev'nin' sun go down." He'd lost his pseudo-British accent and sounded more like the street minstrels of St. Louis, his hometown. "Well?" he asked with a grin.

Viv clapped her hands in delight. "Oh, Tom! You're my dashing American again!" She hugged him.

"I think being here in Margate by the sea has reminded me of Gloucester where my family summered, and that, in its turn, reminded me of St. Louis. Whether in my backyard or out for a stroll with my nurse, Annie, I would hear blues music coming from some of the saloons or from street musicians playing on corners or in parks. This song, called "St. Louis Blues", was popular, so I heard it everywhere and, without realizing, learned it completely," Tom remembered fondly.

"Get up, Viv!" he said, standing and offering his hand to her. "We're going to dance."

"But, Tom, there's no music." Even so, Vivien stood to be taken into Tom's arms.

"I'll be the band," he said confidently. "One, two, three!" he counted out the beat, then sang, including sounding out the tempo beats, all of "St. Louis Blues," explaining to Vivien between breaths as he twirled her carelessly through their room, "This is the habanera rhythm imitating the tango style of Cuba." His dancing was a perfect blend of leading her

masterfully through the steps and pausing dramatically as he held her stationary in a strong embrace.

When they ended the dance, falling on the bed laughing, Tom said, "I love music and dance, Viv. I love the sound and movement punctuated with silences of great meaning."

"Which I often hear in your poetry, darling." She stared up at the ceiling. "I'm sorry that I have to return to London tomorrow. But I think these two weeks have been good, Tom, really quite good."

"And I am required by doctor's orders to stay another two weeks all alone," he answered, frowning. "Shall we spend our last hours together in wild abandon?" He laughed and turned toward Vivien.

She would not ruin the night that she'd waited so long for. She let Tom, in his shy and hesitant way, determine the course of their love-making that night.

When Vivien left, she made him laugh when she said, "I don't think I'll ever really like your American jazz or blues, Tom. I still prefer a good concerto or ballet. But I'll never forget our tango."

Tom moved to a smaller room at the hotel, budgeting himself economically for the next two weeks. He had brought to Margate a sheaf of papers that comprised his yet-unfinished "long poem" but set it aside until Vivien returned to London. Once she was gone, he spent each day contemplating the poem, writing and rewriting, editing and revising, creating and destroying.

The Albemarle was technically not in Margate but in Cliftonville, east of Margate. It is not on the beach directly, but the sea can be viewed easily from its front-facing rooms. Tom's choice, each day, was to walk right to the cliffs of Botany Bay or left to Margate proper, where there was a shelter in which he could sit facing the sea and either work on his poem (along with a pen, its pages stuffed in his pocket) or—if he brought it— practice his mandolin.

He sat in the Margate shelter watching the tide roll in

and out, soothed by the low rumble of the surf and attuned to the seagulls crying far out by the water. The mandolin lay idle in his lap; he had just finished playing the scales and was thinking of what he might be able to recreate besides "St. Louis Blues." He wanted something gay and carefree to buoy his spirits.

Before Viv left, they'd made love gently and sweetly, as Tom had planned and carefully executed. It was sexually satisfying for Tom but spiritually sad, as if he were admitting to Viv that he could never satisfy her as she wanted or expected, but he loved her nonetheless and would continue to be her faithful companion in whatever ways they decided would be best for them: man and wife? Lovers? Writer and Editor? Of one thing they were sure by the time Vivien left him alone in Margate: they would not be parents, not with each other, probably not ever; Vivien was too saddled with undiagnosed illnesses, and Tom feared that any child they produced would be genetically crippled with her physical and mental shortcomings. That knowledge, those fears, contributed to a caution, a hesitation, in their lovemaking. Margate had made them finally admit their marital incompatibility. It was, Tom realized, quite pitiful, but there was a plus side as well: he was no longer jealous or irate about her inevitable infidelities, and perhaps he could begin, himself, to feel guiltless about his interest in Lottie.

He picked up his mandolin and attempted to pick out the chorus of "The Cubanola Glide":

Once he managed the first eight bars, he only had to remember how to repeat the notes for the remainder of the chorus, which he sang under his breath as he picked out the notes on the strings of the mandolin. Pleased with himself despite quite a few wrong notes, Tom laughed aloud and smiled.

He'd first heard the song just before he left for Paris in 1911. It represented home to him because of that. When he met Viv in 1914, he found a recording of this song to gift her, and he sang it softly in her ear as he taught her the dance itself. After they married and discovered their incompatibility, the song was never played on their victrola again.

Only recently, with Lottie, had the song come back to him. Now, here in Margate, with the sound of the ocean surf and the gulls crying in the background, the melody seemed a perfect counterpoint as he made love to Viv, and she giggled softly when he sang the words in her ear, hugging him tighter and in tempo when he whispered, "Tease, squeeze, lovin' and wooin'. . . ."

Tom put the mandolin aside and opened one of the pages he carried. He took out a pencil, holding its point for a moment against a blank space on the paper. Then he wrote:

> Tease Squeeze lovin
> and wooin
>
> Say, Kid, what're y'
> doin

In his head, he imagined a male voice – his – saying, almost singing, these lines to a beautiful young woman as they strolled down Holyoke Street in Cambridge, Massachusetts. He turns to kiss her but sees it is Viv, who shakes her head and dissipates like smoke. "Lottie!" he says aloud, waking himself up from the moment's daydream. No one is there in the shelter, no one even nearby. He could not recall what in the dream made him utter "Lottie!" but he wondered if he'd been thinking of his mother or the servant girl from the Woolf household.

For a moment, he frightened himself. Was he really getting better here in Margate? It didn't seem possible because of the voices in his head who followed him: imagined voices from his reading, snippets of conversations from pubs and music halls, his mother's words either scolding or disappointed, Vivien's voice in the depths of her illness, too many disparate voices vying for attention from him.

The sheet of paper he'd been writing on lay beside him on the bench, the pencil limp in his open hand. He took up both and wrote: "I can connect nothing with nothing." Folding the page and putting it, with the pencil, into his shirt pocket, he picked up the mandolin and started to walk back to the Albermarle. There was a thin line of perspiration on his upper lip, and a tic had started to pulse in his left eye. "I'll have a cool bath and some dinner," he said to himself. Earlier, he had thought to call Viv at home and play his mandolin to her again; now he believed that a foolish idea; she would probably not even be home.

Conversations with friends decided him that he would not go on to Lady Rothmere's villa, but, on the advice of Ottoline Morrell, someone he trusted, he arranged a month-long stay with Dr. Roger Vittoz in Lausanne, Switzerland. Vittoz was lauded not as a "nerve doctor" but as a "brain doctor" who would help Eliot overcome his *aboulie*. So, Tom packed to return to London for a week; Viv had convinced him that they should spend most of November in Paris before he headed off to Lausanne. Although anxious to get to Vittoz, Tom decided his *aboulie* made him give in to Viv. Nevertheless, he was determined to see Lottie before heading to the Continent again.

Mid-October through Late November 1921

13. Prologue to Lausanne: London without Vivien

The moment Tom stepped off the train in London, his mandolin wrapped in a silk bag and tucked under his arm, he started to feel sick again: dizzy, weak, nauseous with the urban smells and sounds. He retrieved his luggage and took a motor car home.

"I'll get Ellen to prepare all your things for Switzerland, Tom." Vivien took his bags and put them down. "Meanwhile, you need to rest. Lloyd's rang up this morning and said to tell you everything is fine there, and they look forward to your full recovery and return in the new year."

"I felt so much better in Margate, Viv. But London—the noise, the odors, I'm quite overcome." He sat down gently, not unlike an invalid testing his strength.

"Well, I've good news, I think. Mama and Papa need me at their place for a few days, so you won't have to deal with me. Ellen knows how to care for you, and I've phoned Mary Hutchinson to come by at least once a day to sit with you. You like Mary; she'll be great company for you in my absence."

"I thought we would spend time together, Viv." Tom was disappointed.

"Well, you know Papa is still recovering. I think I need to go to them whenever they want." Vivien hesitated, then added, "And Lucy Thayer has agreed to accompany me."

"Lucy? Why do you need Lucy with you?" Tom was immediately suspicious. When Vivien was with Lucy, he knew they always filled their evenings with social events of some sort. "Won't you need to stay with your parents?"

"Of course, silly. But they're in bed by nine. What am I to do all night? Lucy and I will entertain ourselves."

"I don't approve, Viv," Tom said, folding his arms across his chest.

Vivien looked at him, deciding whether or not she would

say what was in her mind: who was he to approve or disapprove of what she wanted to do? She only said, "Please, Tom, it's only a few days. Then, you and I are off to Paris until you have to go to Lausanne."

"Paris?" he asked, brightening.

"Yes, you didn't think I'd leave you to go to the continent alone, did you? I've made arrangements for Paris, and I've already written Ezra and Dorothy to meet us. When you go to Switzerland, I'll stay in Paris in case I'm needed. I'll be just next door, so to speak, darling."

Tom's simmering anger dissipated. "Well, Mary Hutchinson is only a substitute, but I suppose she and I can stand one another for a few days. We'll find something to do, Viv." He smiled. "You do think of everything, dear."

Tom and Vivien had met Mary through Bertie Russell and eventually came to know her better as part of the Bloomsbury Group because of her long-standing affair with Clive Bell. Both she and Clive were married—she to a lawyer, he to Vanessa, the sister of Virginia Woolf—but they felt an irresistible sexual attraction to one another. Neither her husband nor Vanessa seemed to mind the affair, and it had been going on for about seven years. Mary was a writer but not well regarded as such by the Bloomsbury Set, and they all thought her more a fashion maven than anything else. Her cousin, Lytton Strachey, encouraged her to wear clothes that Virginia Woolf described as "ravishing." Tom liked her for two reasons: she flouted convention, and she was kinder to Vivien than the others in Bloomsbury. Besides, she enjoyed flirting with him when Vivien wasn't around, and Tom safely flirted back, knowing that she was infatuated with Clive.

Mary would not allow Tom to stay at home feeling sorry for himself because he was ill or because Vivien had left him alone for a few days. She took him to lunch every day, always choosing a place where they were sure to meet acquaintances with whom they shared lunch and gossip. At tea time, she appeared at his apartment with some pastry or biscuit. Then, before leaving around five, she would reveal that she'd planned something for the evening, and she'd pick him up at eight.

Tom barely had the time or inclination to pity himself or to feel ill. He was always tired, usually falling asleep between Mary's visits, whether he was reading or trying to write. He couldn't focus on his tasks and, worse, didn't care. He let Mary direct his life as she required. He enjoyed his outings with her, but it was an empty enjoyment, momentary and without lasting effect. The minute Mary would drop him off at home and close the door, his smile would involuntarily disappear and his *aboulie* return.

After three days and nights of being attended to by Mary, Tom begged her for a quieter event for the next to last night before Vivien returned. Mary decided that a late afternoon visit to the Woolfs would be just the thing: a calm, intellectual evening in their cozy salon where they could drink, smoke, and philosophize as long as they'd like. Tom could hardly hide his excitement: he would see Lottie again.

When they arrived at Hogarth House, Virginia and Leonard greeted them warmly and effusively. The four of them settled in the parlor, and Mary said, "I'm surprised there is no one else here, Virginia. Your house is so often a hive of activity."

"Having heard of Tom's difficulty, I decided a quiet time with us might be best," Virginia answered. She thought Tom looked marmoreal, and she added, "Tom, I hope you can relax a bit here."

"A whiskey would certainly help," he answered, smiling thinly.

Leonard went to the doorway. "Mr. Higgins," he called, "could you bring in the liquor cart?"

Mary sat on one side of Tom and Virginia on the other, as if the two women were his nursemaids caring for him. Leonard remained standing and lit his pipe.

"Vivien is with her parents; her father is still recuperating. And I've been appointed Tom's caretaker," Mary said.

"I'm glad," Virginia said, patting Tom's hand. "Your wife

is showing her parents due respect; it's a wonderful gesture."

"Yes," Tom murmured and nodded. He was unusually quiet and lethargic.

Mary put her arm on his shoulder and leaned in. "You're right, Tom. A strong drink will do wonders for your constitution." She laughed lightly.

They heard the cart, usually kept in a small pantry off the hall, being wheeled down the hall toward them. Suddenly, the front of the cart, bottles rattling on its shelf, appeared in the doorway. It was pushed into the room by Lottie. "Mr. 'iggins said to bring this," she said shyly as she pushed the cart into a corner. She did not dare look at Tom while everyone watched her set up her station.

"Whiskies all around, Lottie, please," Leonard instructed. "you pour, dear girl, and I'll serve."

Mary laughed again. "Does no one want tea?" She was making a joke to diminish the sense of doom that Tom had brought into the room.

"We'll drink," Virginia pronounced, "then we'll have something light to eat." She took her drink from Leonard. "Thank you, darling." She turned to Mary. "Then, you shall go, whether to your husband or your lover I care not, but tonight Tom and I, with Leonard's agreement, will use the theatre tickets I have." She turned to Tom. "I will not take no for an answer."

Mary nodded and squeezed Tom's shoulder. "I agree, and so shall you." Mary had long suspected that Virginia, like herself, harbored a secret physical attraction to Tom, which neither would ever reveal unless Tom encouraged it. Once, Virginia asked her, as if simply daydreaming, "At what point, Mary, do you think copulation is necessary to friendship with men?" Mary laughed at first but was, from that moment forward, suspicious of Virginia's motives whenever she gave her attention to men other than Leonard, particularly Tom, who obviously basked in the attention lavished on him but also managed to keep all flirtations superficial. Was that the source of his allure, she wondered, his seeming inviolability? She shook her head. We women always want what we cannot have.

"I'm glad to spend a quiet evening at home," Leonard said, handing a drink to Mary and another to Tom.

"Thank you all for your prescriptions," Tom said. "May I take a moment alone to contemplate my decision?"

"Oh, Tom, just say yes," Mary answered. "Besides, where can you be alone, and why would you want to?"

"I'll step out on the pavement if none of you mind." He drained his glass in a single gulp.

"Well, don't take too much time. And don't disappoint us, Tom," Leonard said, "I would really like to stay home alone tonight."

Tom moved to the doorway. He stopped a moment and turned back to the room. "Virginia, would you send Lottie here after me with a shawl or blanket? There's a bit of a chill in the air." He didn't wait for an answer but disappeared from the room. They heard him open and close the front door.

"That damned fool," Virginia muttered. "he'll catch pneumonia if not influenza. Lottie, get a shawl from Leonard's room and bring it to Mr. Eliot."

"He'll come 'round," Mary said. "We both know he just adores the attention we pay him. He just likes to be dramatic."

As Lottie moved to leave, Virginia said, "Lottie, before you bring the shawl to Mr. Eliot, tell cook there will be four for a light supper at seven. Our tickets are for nine."

"Yes, Mrs. Woolf," Lottie said. She smiled sweetly.

Out on the street, Tom stood leaning on a lamppost, smoking a cigarette. It was around five-thirty, and in November, dusk was already settling on the scene. When he saw Lottie coming through the front door, he straightened and smiled.

"Mrs. Woolf told me to bring you this shawl, Mr. Eliot," Lottie said, pressing the shawl against his chest and glancing nervously back at the windows of Hogarth House.

Tom laughed and pulled her close to him. "You're so sweet, Lottie," he said breathlessly. "And don't fret. They cannot see us from the parlor: its windows face only the side of the house. We could kiss here if we wanted." He smiled at her. "And I so want to."

Lottie wriggled out of his arms. "Not 'ere," she mumbled. "Let me 'elp you, though," she added, opening the shawl and attempting to throw it over his shoulders.

Tom helped her to wrap the shawl around him. "You are the only spark of fire in my life, Lottie," he whispered. "I am so cold and sick of this world." He pulled the shawl tight around himself and sighed. He looked like he was going to cry.

Lottie showed confusion on her face. She wanted to help him, but she was frightened of him, too. "I ain't never met a man like you, so open with 'is feelings like," she said, stepping back from him. "I want to 'elp you, but what can I do?"

Tom brightened momentarily. "Can you slip out late tonight, around eleven?"

"Oh, sir, I'm a-bed by eleven most nights." Lottie shook her head.

"I've have you a-bed by midnight the latest," Tom responded, assuring her. When she only looked quizzically at him, he added, "You must come to my place. I'll give you carfare."

"Your—your wife, sir?" Lottie looked shocked.

"Possum's wife is away, so possum can play," Tom answered as if he were reciting a rhyme to a child. "It's easy to remember: 9 Clarence Gate Gardens." He pressed a 5£ note into her hand.

"I didn't say I could come," Lottie said, holding the money limply.

"You didn't say you wouldn't. I'll wait up for you, Lottie." Eliot turned away and headed back into Hogarth House trailing the edges of the shawl behind him.

After dinner, during which Tom demonstrated more animation than he had since he and Mary had arrived at the Woolfs', Mary said she'd like to see Clive and would leave Tom in the "capable hands of Virginia and Leonard."

"I do believe that this supper has reinvigorated me, at least temporarily," Tom announced. "Mary, go to Clive. I'm actually looking forward to a night out with Virginia. Leonard, I promise to send her home immediately after the last curtain."

Leonard shook his head. "Tom, no one sends Virginia anywhere. I thought you'd understood that by now."

Outside the theater, the performance over, Tom and Virginia were waiting in a queue for cabs and talking about Tom's work as a reviewer. When Virginia was getting into her cab to return to Hogarth House, Tom checked his watch: ten-thirty. He smiled. The last thing he said to Virginia that night was, "The critics say I am learned and cold. The truth is I am neither."

14. Prologue to Lausanne: London with Lottie

Tom arrived back at Clarence Gate Gardens at ten minutes to eleven, just enough time to warm the rooms against the November cold. He turned on the lights in the dining room, revealing a table crowded with books, papers, and the newer Corona typewriter his brother had left him. In the parlor, he turned on only a table lamp that provided a small, warm circle of yellowish light on the divan. He closed the door to Vivien's bedroom, then, in his own bedroom, turned on the bedside lamp. He smoothed the sheets and duvet carefully, glad that the bed had been redressed. It was narrow, but he thought it a good excuse to hold Lottie close to him. He retrieved a heavy towel and laid it inconspicuously on the bottom sheet under the duvet.

At eleven, the mantle clock in the dining room chimed softly. Tom had removed his suit jacket and hung it in his wardrobe. Now, he removed his watch and its fob from his vest pocket and laid them on the table. He drummed his fingers impatiently. Would she actually *not* appear?

Ten minutes later, a soft knock at the door. Tom rose quickly, straightened his vest and his hair, and opened the door. He pulled her by the arm into the apartment. Only then did he hug her. "I am so glad to see you," he said.

"I told Cook I was feelin' poorly and needed a stroll," Lottie said. "I'm sure she didn't believe me, but let me go anyway."

"We'll have you back for morning tasks, bright and early," Tom assured her.

"Morning?" Lottie asked incredulously.

"You will stay with me this night," Tom insisted. "I could not go to Paris or Lausanne without a memory of you sleeping in my arms."

"But, I—" Lottie trembled. "I'm a good girl, Possum," she stated almost indignantly. Now that the moment had arrived, she was not so certain that she wanted their relationship to be consummated.

Tom held her at arms' length, much like a schoolteacher would hold a student on whom a lesson must be impressed. "I'll be gentle and careful, Lottie, I promise. You must let me show you how wonderful it can be between a man and a woman."

"And after?" Lottie asked in a small, frightened voice.

"After? You will have a wonderful memory, Lottie, of your first love. You will treasure every moment of it in recollection. And, I assure you, the experience will make you so much more attractive to men who will compete for your affections until one of them wins your heart forever. This is your moment, Lottie, and I am so glad to be the one to give it to you." Then, Tom kissed her briefly and said, " Let's have a whiskey, then let me show you the bedroom, and afterwards, we could have a spot of tea before we sleep." He led her to the divan.

Tom was nervous, but not in the way that his nerves had suffered these past months. This was the anxiety of anticipation, and the whiskey—he downed three in quick succession and demanded that Lottie have one—eased the anxiety. He kept Lottie on the divan while he caressed her, his fingertips alert to feeling when her tension was draining, and the surface of her skin felt warm and yielding. He unbuttoned her top and caressed her breasts. He pushed up her skirt and felt for the touch of flesh beneath her underclothes. He leaned his weight against her as he explored her with his hands and tongue. He was, as he had planned, the most gentle of lovers.

In the bedroom, he extinguished the light, in deference to her hesitation and timidity, and helped her to undress in the dark. He turned down the duvet and allowed her to cover herself with it while he hurried to undress himself. He shed all his clothes onto the floor, eager to join Lottie in the warm bed. He was confident that the darkness would hide his hernias. For a moment, when he first got on top of her, a vision of rude ravishing flashed in his mind: Pan cackling and hotly mounting his conquest, but almost immediately, when he looked into Lottie's large, frightened eyes, he felt a rush of concern, of gentleness, for the girl, and he remembered all the poignant scenes he'd read of romantic, tender embracing. "You're so lovely, Lottie," he whispered, tempering his excitement with kindness.

After, he gave Lottie his bathrobe, put on his own pajamas, and settled her briefly on the divan while he made tea. In the cozy yellow circle of light, he asked, "Are you all right?"

She sipped loudly at the cup of steaming tea. "It only hurt for a moment, Possum."

"In the future, it will be more wonderful than tonight, I am sure. You are a sweet girl, Lottie, always remember that."

"Will I have your child?" she asked innocently.

"We hope not," he answered. "If it should come to that," he added offhandedly, "ask Cook to help you. I'm sure she will know how to deal with the situation." Tom felt no pang of guilt or responsibility about this; he believed as he was taught and told: if a sexual encounter resulted in pregnancy, it was the woman's responsibility to deal with it. Even though he told himself that he loved Lottie, he knew that any relationship with her other than purely clandestine was out of the question. He believed she understood that as well. "I will not, however," he continued, "put you in the situation of being my mistress, Lottie. I am married, of course, and intend to remain faithful to my vows if not actually to my wife."

Lottie watched him surreptitiously over the rim of her teacup. The deed was done, she thought, no use crying over it now. She had agreed to this, even wanted it. And he was no brute, she thought, unlike what other girls had said some men were like forcing themselves on the girl without regard for feelings or expectations, then either turning over and snoring away the rest of the night or getting up and out of the girl's life forever after. No, here she was with Possum in his place, having tea and sitting in his robe, which smelled of him and his cologne. She had no regrets; he'd never said he would leave his marriage for her, after all.

After tea, Tom collected the dishes and brought them

into the kitchen. When he returned, he surprised Lottie by scooping her up in his arms and carrying her into the bedroom. He deftly pulled the towel in the bed to the floor and laid Lottie down on the cool sheets. He covered her gently with the duvet and kissed her forehead. "Try to sleep, dear girl. You have given me such joy."

Tom sat on the edge of the bed and waited. When he was sure that she was indeed fast asleep, he gathered his clothes and threw them into the bottom of the wardrobe, and carried the bloodied towel into the kitchen where he stuffed it into the cooking stove onto the simmering coals. It was two a.m.; by morning, the towel would be nothing more than a layer of ashes.

Since the next day was Sunday, Tom believed that he could wake Lottie as late as five a.m. to get her dressed and back to Hogarth House for her chores. She'd be at her duties by six or seven at the latest. From having spent weekends with the Woolfs, he knew they liked to start their day later on Sundays—around eight—so Lottie wouldn't really be missed. And, once she was gone, he could make sure to erase any trace of her before Vivien returned.

When he put Lottie in a cab at five-thirty a.m., the motor's engine steaming in the early morning air, he made no promises to her, and she asked for none. "I'm sure we will meet again, Lottie," he said, knowing that he'd certainly see her during any future visits to the Woolfs'.

"Yes, Possum, I'm sure." Lottie smiled wistfully. "I hope you have a grand time in Paris and Switzerland, Mr. Eliot," she said bravely. Addressing him by his surname was her acknowledgement of the nature of their relationship.

"You've grown up so," Tom said, shaking his head. "I never intended to hurt you, Lottie. You know that, right?"

Lottie nodded and pulled the cab door closed. She wanted him to see that she had not been disappointed, that she still cared for him.

When Tom went back inside, he tidied up the apartment carefully, making sure that Lottie's presence would not be detected because Vivien would be returning the next day. While he was straightening his bed, however, he could still smell the lovely odor of her lavender scent on his pillow. He laid down in his bed with the pillow held to his nose.

He had no doubt that he had been the perfect lover: never rushing, always attentive to Lottie's responses as he kissed and caressed her, and finally deflowering her as gently as possible, managing to control his sexual urgency. It had not only been successful, he thought, but perfectly executed. He was the man he always imagined himself to be when he daydreamed at Harvard about losing his virginity. Lottie was completely compliant but also appreciative. She seemed to participate in their love-making, kissing him back, embracing him tightly, and smiling when he smiled at her. There was nothing sordid in that experience.

It was not that way with Vivien. Perhaps, he thought, it could have been, but they had rushed into their relationship—each for their own reasons—and not thought through how they could be successful in their marriage. He'd made a mess of it, he was sure.

These thoughts partially drained away his feelings of well-being. Now, alone in the apartment, about to go to Paris where he was sure, Ezra would rip apart whatever he'd already written of his long poem, knowing that Vivien would see Paris as *her* escape from their problems and worried about how things would turn out with Vittoz in Lausanne, Tom started to shake again. It was as if his rendezvous with Lottie had happened long ago, not yesterday and its memory could not sustain in him a sense of peace and serenity.

Tom looked at the papers piled on the dining room table. Some were typescript, others written in bold black ink, and still others with pencil markings. The books were of various thicknesses and colors, most with slips of paper dangling from them to mark pages and passages for him. The Corona typewriter sat sturdily in front of his chair. He touched it gently, remembering again how kind it was of his brother to take Tom's dilapidated typewriter and replace it with his own newer one. The ribbon was not fresh but still dark, unlike the one on Tom's typewriter, which was so used that it was almost transparent in places.

Tom ran his fingers across the keys of the Corona. He meant to chuckle ironically, to indicate that he understood his brother's generosity despite his disapproval, but instead, the sound he made was a choking sob. His life was a mess, he thought. A loveless marriage. An unresolved dispute with his father, who had died before Tom could prove himself successful on his father's terms. A mother who loved him to smothering and continued to wordlessly demand he do her bidding. A job as a bank clerk, which everyone thought beneath him but which he secretly admitted only to himself, was a great excuse for not being the successful poet he should be. And tonight, taking advantage of a girl's infatuation with him, even if he thinks he loved her.

And why was he so frail, he thought with annoyance. Double hernias since birth. Respiratory illnesses that sent him into coughing fits. Unexplained aches and pains that made him feel ten years older than he was. But, mostly, the mental frailty: an inability, sometimes an unwillingness, to complete a poem or an essay, even a letter or a sentence. A despondence that barely allowed him to get out of bed some days.

At Harvard, he took boxing lessons, was active in a number of societies, and stayed up nights drinking with friends, carousing and disturbing the peace in the early morning hours. Now, he walked with measured steps, engaged in purely intellectual discussions, drank heavily, suffered moments of embarrassing drunkenness in front of friends, and obeyed the law assiduously. He had become *respectable*, an adjective unknown and even unbecoming in describing his French symbolist poet-mentors or even his dear friend, Ezra Pound.

With these realizations at this early Sunday morning hour in his London flat with everyone he cared for far away, he pulled together the pages of his new, still-unfinished poem and determined that it would be the receptacle into which he'd pour all of his unhappiness, making some mystical transference from his soul to its pages.

15. Prologue to Lausanne: Paris

The day after Vivien returned to London from her parents' home, she and Tom were on their way to Paris. "You're still cross with me for leaving you alone in London? I would have thought that Mary was good company."

Tom said nothing right away. Just watched the French countryside from the train window. "I suppose I am, although Mary was quite nice." he finally said. They were in the last three hours of the eleven-hour trip between London and Paris, and he was tired.

"We'll have a splendid time in Paris, Tom. It's your favorite city, you'll get to speak French again, and we'll have Dorothy and Ezra in the company. It will be perfect." Vivien smiled brightly and looked out the window. "This countryside is not quite as nice, however, as England."

Tom almost said, "It's you being here that spoils it all, Vivien," but just lowered his head. Why am I so irritable? he wondered. But he knew that he was wishing he were with Lottie rather than Vivien, and he was now anxious to get to Lausanne and get his treatment with Vittoz underway. "I think Vittoz will really help me," he said, changing the subject.

"Oh, Tom, he's not English. How can you trust someone who doesn't understand the English—or, for that matter, American—character?" Vivien argued, shaking her head at her husband in disbelief.

"Both Julian Huxley and Ottoline Morrell recommend him highly. I've read his book, Vivien. It's called *Traitment des psychonèvroses,* and it makes some really excellent points about controlling one's mind to achieve health." He started to rummage for the book in the bag next to him.

"Really, Tom, he's French," Vivien said, a statement of dismissal.

"It seems, at last," Tom said quietly and ironically, "you and Mother have something in common: a dislike for the

French. She once disapproved of my spending a year in Paris at the Sorbonne." He closed the bag, knowing it was pointless to show the book to Vivien.

"And you sometimes think too highly of the French," Vivien sneered.

They spoke little the rest of the way to Paris, choosing silence to an argument that would be the more unpleasant alternative.

When they arrived at the Hotel Pas-de-Calais in the St. Germain de Pres district, Tom's mood lightened a little because he realized that they were not far from his favorite park, the Luxembourg Gardens. Although Vivien suggested they shop for some essentials, Tom chose to stroll in the park. He took with him a small notebook, hoping to write something about returning to Paris.

He entered the Gardens from the north, skirting the Senate building and heading east toward the *Fontaine Medicis*. With the certainty of a former *Parisien*, he moved around the Medici Fountain to where the lesser-known *Fontaine de Leda* stood. Tom gazed at the fountain: a bas-relief of Leda held in the wings of Zeus disguised as a swan. His slender neck and beaked head are draped across Leda's thighs; the water flows from his mouth. This was Tom's favorite spot, partly hidden from view and less visited than the Medici Fountain against which it rested.

He chuckled at a memory. His friend from student days at the Sorbonne, Jean Verdenal, had explained to him that this fountain was obscured in part by placing the Medici Fountain here: in 1812, the government thought this fountain unsuitable for public display because of its theme, Leda being ravished by Zeus. Tom peered closely at the sculpture.

In the artist's version (Achilles Valois), Leda was not resisting Zeus; in fact, she looked to be enjoying the experience, one arm resting behind her head. Amor, the young cupid, is depicted standing to the left, drawing a love arrow from his quiver. Tom remembered being with Lottie: how, after she had fallen asleep, he had briefly laid his head across her thighs to inhale her scent. For the first time, a woman's odor had not repelled him, and he kissed her skin lightly before he had covered her with the duvet. Tom sighed. One last look at the fountain, and he swung around back to the Medici Fountain.

Tom chose a bench apart, pulled out his pen and notebook, and closed his eyes, listening to the sound of the water flowing. In his mind, he still kept the image of the Leda fountain, then wrote, squinting in the dusky light, "She smooths her hair. . . ." He had not yet decided if the gesture was, as with Lottie, one of self-assurance or, as often was with Vivien, one of unsatisfied boredom. He would not determine that yet, for both Paris and Lausanne still awaited him.

Paris gave both Tom and Vivien a respite from illness, it seemed. They spent their days going to galleries and museums and their evenings at concerts or lectures. Tom wrote little, telling Vivien it was "doctor's orders" to refrain from work. At night, they slept side by side without the usual tension of sexual incompatibility, for they had exhausted themselves sufficiently during the day. In addition, the air in Paris was decidedly clearer than in London, so both felt healthier.

Only twice in three weeks did Tom feel sick: both times, he woke bathed in sweat from a deep sleep, his hands trembling uncontrollably. Both times, he realized he'd been having a dream of Vivien and Bertie Russell coupling urgently, she moaning loudly and he chortling with glee. Once, Tom remembered from the dream, Bertie Russell had turned to face him while still pushing into Vivien and said, "I warned her you were exquisite but listless." A shot of whiskey calmed him enough to return to sleep.

They'd met Ezra and Dorothy for dinner a few times, even spent one late night drinking into the early morning and singing old American pop tunes, but Tom put off spending any "poetic" time with Ezra until he was only a week and a half away from leaving for Lausanne. He finally could not put Ezra off any longer after Dorothy complained to Vivien that "Ezra is wondering why Tom is so distant."

"Tom, let's get it sorted with Ezra, eh?" Vivien said

impatiently.

"There's nothing to work out, Viv; I've just been busy," Tom insisted.

"Busy if you call mucking about busy," she answered.

"You think I'm wasting time, then?" Tom asked, trying to sound annoyed so that Viv would drop the subject.

"I think you don't want Ezra to see your work, afraid he'll be critical and change it; that's what it is, innit?"

"No." Tom hesitated to voice his complaint to Vivien, who, he knew, generally thought highly of Ezra's criticisms of and corrections to his poetry. "I am still working on the poem. I'm not sure it's ready for Ezra's pencil."

In fact, Tom had been avoiding the subject that was the true cause of their dispute: Tom had been raised to believe that public disputes were best settled if wrapped in courtesies and mildness; Ezra preferred a battering-ram approach—that is, apply frontal, overt attacks. Thus, a piece Tom had written in March about poetry for the journal *Tyro* struck Ezra as particularly mealy-mouthed, and he did not refrain from saying so the following month, April, in *The Little Review*. Tom, his emotions fragile and vulnerable, was stung by the criticism, not only because it came from someone he considered a good friend but also because he felt that Ezra had completely misread Tom's primary point.

Now, in Paris, desperate for the cure he thought Vittoz would provide, he had no desire to confront or be confronted by Ezra over this; he felt too weak to defend himself. Further, he had now invested a good deal of time and effort into his long poem, had completed three parts of it, and he actually became nauseous at the thought that Ezra would destroy those three parts in his brutally honest and unforgiving way.

Yet, when the dreaded meeting occurred, Tom found Ezra uncharacteristically gentle, asking only that Tom leave the pages with him to be discussed "after Switzerland" when Tom was back to himself. What comforted Tom the most was Ezra's remark after scanning the various pages that Tom handed him:

"Well, Possum, Ize do think that you have done as Rabbit suggested," he said, imitating the Brer Rabbit speech of the Joel Harris stories, "you has put everythin' into this." Ezra patted Tom's knee, glad to see his friend relaxing into a less guarded posture, "Bravo, Possum."

When Tom left Ezra and Dorothy, both wishing him a successful recovery in Switzerland, and Dorothy even insisting on hugging him tightly and whispering, "Farewell, dear Tom," he headed for the Luxembourg Gardens to sit quietly. He was trembling, exhausted from the expectation of disappointment as well as from the surprise of unqualified support, and he needed to sit alone, away from the crowded, bustling streets of Paris.

Tom realized that Ezra was not only his brilliant editor but also a generous friend who was liberal not only with advice but also with love and support. He blushed with shame that he had not seen this quality in Ezra before and, worse, that he had never reciprocated similarly. He wondered if his adherence to formality—taught to him in the Eliot household—was another symptom of his *aboulie,* which he was now desperate for Vittoz to cure. Tears trickled down his face, although he looked perfectly normal to passersby as long as they gave him no more than a glance.

"Are you sure you don't want to return to London?" he asked Vivien the night before his departure for Lausanne. His bag was packed, now standing by the door of their room. The wardrobe in the room looked forlorn, with half of its contents packed in Tom's valise.

"I'm bloody positive, Tom," Vivien responded with annoyance.

"I'm only concerned about you," he answered. He had planned this last night together carefully, modeling it on the successful night he had with Lottie. First, he intended for her to see that she would miss him. "You're all alone here, except for Ezra and Dorothy. I worry that if you take ill, there is no one for you to turn to."

"First of all, Tom," Vivien said, glaring at him, "I am

perfectly healthy here in Paris, away from the vile air in London. Second, do you think I'm not capable of being by myself? I've done so before you, and I'll do just fine now. And, finally, I will probably not stay in Paris at all during your treatment at Lausanne. I may take some brief holidays elsewhere." She rubbed her palms together as if she'd already decided what to do.

Tom stiffened. "Where?" he asked, choosing to say nothing more that might reveal his sudden anxiety. In a single moment, he realized this would not go as planned. It felt like something was pressing on his chest.

"I don't know, Tom. Lucy's brother, Scofield, is somewhere in Germany, Ottoline's villa is available, I've got loads of options." She shrugged her shoulders.

"I see," Tom said quietly. When they'd started this conversation, he'd been concerned for Vivien. Now, hearing that she'd already seemed to be making plans other than waiting for him, his mind buzzed with speculation about Viv's fidelity. He'd seen her flirt with Scofield many times, but she denied it when he confronted her. She was, she'd say, "being congenial." And his anger with Scofield simmered as well. The man thought himself both irresistible and beyond reproach. More maddening was that Vivien had been sure to tell both Bertie Russell and Scofield Thayer that he, Tom, needed to go to Vittoz. It made him look weak.

"Please, Tom, your departure shouldn't be spoiled with our disagreeing. You must be sure that I'll be fine just as I'll be sure that you will be fine, too."

"I'm certain you'll be fine, Viv," he said. Then, "Let's go out tonight and have a memorable last night together. What do you say?" He smiled weakly.

Vivien glanced sideways at him; he looked pale to her. "All right, Tom, if that's what you want."

What Vivien had not anticipated was that Tom would drink himself into a drunken stupor, starting with dinner, then making sure they stopped at two or three music halls on the way back to the hotel. By the time they'd reached their room, he was barely able to remove his shoes. Vivien had to help him undress and then put him into his pajamas and bed. He snored drunkenly almost as soon as she tucked him in, but not before he said to her, a big grin on his face, "Sorry, Viv, I'm really not in the mood tonight." He had echoed what she often said to him when she wanted him to know he was not desired, even when he made no overture to sex.

The next evening, she waited with Tom at the train for Lausanne. The Gare du Nord was crowded and noisy. Steam rose from the engines just arrived, and those anxious to depart, people clustered on the platforms, checking the time and hovering over their luggage. "Are you feeling better?" Vivien asked, her arm looped inside Tom's.

"I'll be fine to sleep on the train, I'm sure," Tom said noncommittedly.

"I know you drank too much to avoid me last night, Tom." She did not want him to leave with a lie, no matter how comforting, between them.

"I drank to facilitate your avoiding me, Viv," Tom answered bitterly.

"I'll be in Paris in case you need me, Tom," she said, ignoring his remark.

"So," Tom couldn't help himself, "does this mean you won't be headed to Germany or elsewhere to be comforted while I'm in Lausanne?"

The conductor rang a loud handbell. "*A Lausanne sur la voie cinq, Dix minutes avant le départ.*" His voice echoed through the station.

"I've got to go, Viv," Tom said, removing Vivien's arm from his. "I'll wire my address and phone number." He stepped up onto the train, clearly ignoring the cheek she offered for a departing kiss.

Vivien, hesitating for a moment between sadness and anger, finally decided on wrath. "Don't fret, Tom, I won't go to Germany. I'll make sure that I entertain visitors *here* instead."

She smiled bitterly and turned away.

Tom watched her go, almost called out to her, then shrugged his shoulders. "All for the poem, Ezra, I promise, all for the poem," he whispered and shook his head. He retreated into the train to check on his valise.

December 1921

16. Lausanne, at last

During winter, the early morning hours were still dark in Lausanne. When Tom left the train station, valise filled with clothes and papers in hand, this last week in November, he noted the cold silence of the town at dawn but could not see the magnificent panorama of the Alps through the clouds.

Despite the icy weather, the waters of Lake Geneva (*Lac Léman* to the French) lapped so softly on the shores that it was hardly noticeable. Some days, the brisk winds out of the Alps threw the lake's waters up into angry waves, especially in winter, but in general, Lausanne's relationship with Lake Geneva was a calm and serene one. It was just what Tom needed in terms of a healing environment.

He checked in at the Hotel Sainte Luce, a modest guest house, happy to have secured the same room once rented by Ottoline Morrell. The hotel was not only relatively close to the train station but also convenient to the center of town as well as, most importantly, near the residence and office of Dr. Vittoz, whom he was to see that very afternoon.

Tom was superstitious enough to believe that being in the same room as Ottoline might bring him the same peace that she enjoyed after her sessions with Vittoz. He wanted, above all, to simply be *well*, a condition which he believed would be the basis for his success as a writer. The room was simple but *gemütlich:* a bed with a thick boiled green wool blanket, an old stuffed chair with frayed arms, and a simple desk in the corner. A single lamp on the desk provided light at night; during the day, the cold, strong sunlight bathed the room in brightness. A scuffed wooden wardrobe was squeezed into a corner; it could only be opened or closed if the room's main door were shut. Tom thought the room a splendid place to be cured.

He had arrived in Lausanne early enough to have breakfast in the guest house dining room, and he looked forward to eating a freshly-prepared meal before presenting himself to Vittoz. Perhaps other guests knew something about the doctor. Tom remained in his travel clothes except for his collar and tie, which he exchanged for new ones from his valise.

Downstairs (Tom's room was on the first floor), he was greeted with smiles and salutations, although he had to accustom himself to the slower pace of Swiss French and to some of its peculiar accenting. Seating him at a small table against a wall, the young waitress explained to him that they had for *dejuner* both croissants and baguettes as well as coffee and tea. Realizing that the Swiss French had abbreviated *petit dejuner* (breakfast) to just *dejuner*, he ordered a baguette and tea. The dining room, occupying a ground floor corner of the house, looked out both on the main street and on breathtaking views of the Lac Leman and, if there were no cloud cover, the Alps beyond. Tom's first sight of the lake—huge, glassy, rippling with winter wind—made him catch his breath. *Magnifique*, he mouthed without speaking, even though the winter morning's mist still hid his view of the Alps beyond the lake.

He had brought Vittoz's book with him to breakfast, so while he drank his tea and broke off bite-size chunks of the freshly-baked baguette to savor, he thumbed through the book, stopping to review passages he had already underlined or marked with a asterisk. He glanced at his watch; the appointment with Vittoz was now less than fifteen minutes away. Tom sighed contentedly, rubbed some crumbs off his fingertips, and finished his tea. "*Merci*," he said as he walked past the waitress. He intended to return to his room to stow away Vittoz's book and to comb and brilliantine his hair, paying special attention to a razor-sharp part.

It was a very short walk from the hotel to Roger Vittoz's residence, where the doctor had set apart a parlor as his office. The doctor himself, twenty-five years the senior of Tom, was meticulous about his appearance: traditional three-piece suit, sensible but highly-polished shoes, a simple shirt with starched collar and a solid gray bowtie. His brush moustache projected stability and authority to Tom.

"*Asseyez-vous s'il vous plait*," Vittoz said, motioning to a comfortable club chair, seating himself in a more formal straight-back wooden chair.

"*Merci beaucoup*." Tom sat down gently on the edge of the chair, squaring his shoulders rather than relaxing into the cushions. He was relieved that Vittoz's French, although Swiss in origin, was understandable to him.

"Before we speak of you in particular, Mr. Eliot, may I ask if you know something about my therapy?" Vittoz folded his hands in his lap.

"Yes, Doctor. I've read your book, and I've also spoken to two of your former patients who recommended you without qualification, Mrs. Ottoline Morrell and Mr. Julian Huxley. I am certain that your methods will help me, even cure me." Eliot leaned forward, his earnestness and eagerness clear in his expression.

"Ah," Vittoz answered with a smile, "but surely you will leave the diagnosis and prognosis to me?" He patted Tom's knee.

"Oh, but of course," Tom said hastily. "I didn't mean that I—I would not presume—" he stammered and blushed.

"It's all right. I just want to be assured that you are already familiar with my method of treatment. Let's speak of you now, please." Vittoz removed from his suit jacket a small pad and pencil as well as his pince-nez, which he perched expertly on the bridge of his nose.

Tom's shoulders sagged under the stress of this first meeting. "*Aboulie*," he said, sighing.

"I suffer a lack of will." He lowered his head and closed his eyes. A tiny trembling started in his hands, and he had lain flat on his knees.

"That you recognize it, Mr. Eliot," Vittoz said soothingly, "and that you are now sitting here for help—these indicate that you, in fact, have not completely lost your will. It brought you to beautiful Lausanne, no?" Vittoz quickly wrote something in his notepad.

Eliot folded one hand over the other. The trembling subsided, and he nodded.

"Please tell me your specific symptoms as much as you can remember. It will help me to design a treatment just for you." Vittoz put down the pad. "Do you smoke?" He pulled a pack of cigarettes from his pocket, offering one to Tom.

"Thank you, yes," Tom said, grateful for the offer. He pulled a lighter from his own pocket, lit his cigarette, then leaned forward to light Vittoz's. For a moment, they were silent, watching the smoke curl upward toward the ceiling. "I frequently shake and sometimes have a sudden paralysis in my hands. I feel a tightness in my chest, a tingling in my fingers." Tom hesitated and blushed. "I am repulsed by the thought of being embraced by my wife. Less often, I think I can smell her femininity, and I become nauseous."

Vittoz hid his surprise at Tom's admission of sexual dysfunction; it was not one of the usual characteristics of *aboulie*. Vittoz chose his words carefully: "Aside from your wife, do you otherwise love?" The awkward construction of the question was intentional, and Vittoz carefully watched Tom's face.

First, Tom looked down and to the left. "Of course, my family, my brother," he said, then looked down and right, "especially my dear mother." He closed his eyes.

"So, you have loved your family. That is normal, yes?" Vittoz asked quietly. Vittoz was trained in neurology, so he could see from Tom's eye movements that he was recalling emotional memories and feelings.

"Yes, of course," Tom confirmed. He opened his eyes, then unconsciously looked to the right. "We have always been quite close and supportive of each other." He blinked.

"Any others?" Vittoz asked quietly. He noted Tom's eye movements in his notepad, printing the words *constructed not remembered*.

Tom's eyes drifted to the left, then upwards. "Yes, friends, of course. Very close friends." Tom was picturing Ezra, hearing his voice as they spoke of poetry, then Lottie, remembering her sweet reticence, then surrender. Involuntarily, he smiled.

Vittoz made another note: *recalled close friends*. Then,

he stood up. "May I come closer, Mr. Eliot?"

"Yes, of course." Tom's mind snapped back to the present.

"I'm going to put my hands on your head. Please don't be alarmed. Sit back and try to relax."

Tom repositioned himself in the chair so that he was in a more casual posture. He laid his hands at his sides.

"Continue to think of those friends you love, who love you," Vittoz said, placing his hands at Tom's temples and on the crown of his head. His touch was warm and tender, not probing so much as *receiving*, like a conduit gently pulling from Tom's brain all its stoniness.

Tom closed his eyes, but even behind his eyelids, his eyes rolled upwards and to the left, which Vittoz noted. His fingers on Tom's skin were like an extremely slow-motion massage, coaxing the kinks in Tom's brain to dissolve.

Vittoz continued, "Now, see the sign for infinity in your brain. Trace it with your eyes very slowly and deliberately. Carefully. You want the tracing to be accurate." Vittoz's hands repeated in movements at Tom's temples the infinity sign; it soothed him.

It was a minute—less than a minute—that Tom imagined the symbol completed. When he opened his eyes, he felt calmer, his body drained of stress. Noticing a shaft of sunlight coming through a window, he smiled as if he could feel its warmth.

Vittoz sat back in his chair, made a final note in his pad, and closed it. "How do you feel, Mr. Eliot?"

"Quite calm, sir," Tom replied, still smiling. "As if," he said sheepishly, "your hands withdrew something cold and unyielding from my brain."

"Nothing of the sort, I assure you," Vittoz said, laughing. "I touch you not to cure you but to understand through touch how your brain is processing your emotions."

Feeling a clarity he had recaptured from a lost part of himself, Tom said, "What we intend, doctor, is not always the only meaning to be derived from something. I've learned that about poetry, and I daresay it may be applied to all human experiences."

"Perhaps, Mr. Eliot," Vittoz answered and leaned forward to touch Tom's knees. "But I caution you that you must not tax yourself just yet with your normally complex thoughts. Allow me to prescribe simple steps to recovery. You must, for a few days, only allow your mind to deal with basics: shapes, simple arithmetic problems, the formation of words as if composing them visually letter by letter."

"But, I am capable of—" Tom interjected.

"—Of becoming overwhelmed once again. Please, Mr. Eliot, I insist you surrender yourself to my care." Vittoz was less amiable in making this demand. "For the next two weeks, you must come here every day for an hour. I assure you this will be most beneficial."

When Tom left Vittoz to return to his room, it was past lunchtime. He asked that a small soup and salad be brought to his room, where he intended to remain until his next appointment in two days. Meanwhile, Vittoz had directed him to spend at least three hours a day in the mental exercises he described: visual pictures that Tom was to slowly create in his mind. To be so occupied left little room for Tom to feel either stressed or desolate; he was too busy following Vittoz's directives. And, as well, he was delighted to find himself spending his nights writing, revising, editing, rewriting more of his long poem.

17. Lausanne, The Cure

By the middle of December, having been in Lausanne for three weeks and his treatment with Vittoz reduced from daily to every other day, Tom began to think it was time to leave for Paris to rendezvous with Vivien.

Here, he had fallen into a routine: he started each day with a brief mental exercise to settle his thoughts, then breakfast, then back to his room to write and edit. The simple continental breakfasts, in contrast to his usual heavier British breakfast of eggs, sausage, beans, toast, and tea, suited him; he felt lighter and more energetic. His writing came easily, almost automatically, and he had already produced—including edits and revisions of previous poetry—around three hundred lines of his long poem, six times more than he had created in Margate.

He opted for a relatively heavy lunch at noon because he knew that dinner would not be served until eight hours later. He ate slowly and deliberately, sometimes still wrestling in his mind with some lines of poetry that he'd worked on earlier, sometimes doing one of Vittoz's exercises of slowly recreating in his head some words. He found that if he chose what he came to call "good words" like *love, hope*, or *salvation*, he felt clear, calm, and refreshed afterwards.

After lunch, he took long walks, always observant of his surroundings, which he thought he could use in his poem. In particular, he listened to conversations as they drifted past him or as he became acquainted with other visitors.

In a small café near the shore of the lake—its outdoor tables encircled with a clear glass greenhouse—Tom sometimes took a demitasse around three. The strong, bitter coffee reminded him of his student days in Paris, a time from which he could draw sharply-remembered memories not only of scents (fresh baguettes, Spring lilacs, bitter Galoises) but also the varied tones and voices of people. Engaged in such reminiscence one day, Tom was distracted by a woman's voice.

"Are you French? From Paris?"

Tom turned to face the voice, middle-aged with a slight tremolo and heavily accented. Russian, Tom thought. "No, madame, *seulement une fois un etudiant a Sorbonne.*" Tom smiled gently.

"Ah, excuse me. I thought—" she pointed to his coffee, "the demitasse. Only the French and Italian like their coffee like that, I've observed." She was handsome in a matronly way, clothed quite grandly. She had an aperitif in front of her.

Tom stood briefly and bowed. "Tom Eliot, from London," he said. He sat again but turned his chair to face the woman.

"Oh, *enchanté*," she answered, nodding. "I am Alexandra Tegleva." She said her name as if she expected Tom to recognize it. She put out her gloved hand, expecting Tom to kiss it.

Tom looked at the soft, thin white leather, then stood again, bent over, and brushed his lips on the proffered glove. He would not soon forget the smell of that leather, rich like cream, vaguely gamey. He sat down again. "I'm sorry. I believe you're a Russian émigré?"

She nodded. Then, she held an embroidered hanky to her nose as if stifling a short sob and whispered, "*Oui.* I am what you English call a white émigré. I have been in Lausanne since 1920."

Tom, sensing her unfamiliarity with English, continued their conversation in French. "Oh, madame, I am most honored to meet you. I've read in the papers about Russia's troubles. May I offer you another aperitif?" Tom signaled the waiter to replenish the lady's drink as well as to bring him one as well. He recognized the fruity sweetness of Aperol, more pungent because it was poured over ice rather than mixed with soda; for some reason, it made him think of Lottie. He shook his head as if to clear that thought. "Are you happy in Lausanne?" he asked.

"Of course," she insisted immediately. "My husband, Pierre Gilliard, is French. The weather here reminds us of St. Petersburg, where we met." She paused only a moment. "He was the French tutor to the Imperial family and I, the nursemaid to the Imperial Household. Of course, we had to flee.

. . ." her voice trailed off, and she looked into the distance across the lake.

Tom leaned forward. He wanted to pat her shoulder, a gesture of sympathy, but restrained himself. Instead, he simply whispered, "A disgrace what was done to the Romanovs."

"I was so fond of Maria and Anastasia," Tegleva agreed. "*C'est dommage.* They so enjoyed frolicking in the snow."

They spoke little after that, each retreating into their own thoughts while they sipped their aperol. Tom was remembering a German woman he'd met in Munich as a student: Countess Marie Larisch, an outcast from the Austrian Royal Court. She, too, had spoken of sledding in the snow (". . . with my cousin," she had said, "the Crown Prince Rudolph").

When he thought it acceptable, he expressed his farewells and headed back to the hotel. Supper would be served in an hour.

In his room, Tom removed his suit jacket, tie, and stiff collar before stretching out on his bed. The accidental meeting with Alexandra Tegleva made him pensive. When they had been talking in the café, the Russian lilt of her voice made him think of children laughing as they sledded in the snow.

So much had happened to him up to this point, so much that would not have occurred had he stayed in America to become a mediocre (he was sure) philosophy professor. Perhaps, he thought, he would have enlisted and fought in the War. He did not think he would have been injured or died or even that he would have ever been sent into battle; he was sure that he would have distinguished himself in Intelligence services, given his fluency in French and German. But the War, as he experienced it from London, had changed not just him but his entire generation. So many died, so many were maimed. Worst of all, so many had experienced mental derangements. Tom felt sure that at least some part of his own neurasthenia was war-related.

And the influenza. It had swept through Europe with the virulence of the historic Black Death of the Fourteenth Century.

Called "The Spanish Flu," this influenza attacked even healthy people and, in 1918, killed around two million more than the War had. It frightened and worried Tom more than the War had because it was a nearer threat. Besides, it lingered and continued to threaten the health and lives of everyone; as far as Tom knew, his friend Virginia Woolf was still in bed with the influenza, her delicate constitution dangerously weak.

Remembering Virginia reminded him of Lottie. How was the darling girl? He dared not write to her, thereby revealing their secret relationship. He didn't care if Vivien knew; in fact, he almost wished to throw it in her face as his response to her adultery. But, to reveal his dalliance with Lottie to Virginia or Mary Hutchinson, no, that was unthinkable. Lottie was lovely, young, attractive, but a *servant,* after all. His social set would shrug at the idea that Lottie were simply a moment's fancy for him, but a 'relationship'? No, they would think him truly deranged.

As it was, he knew most people thought his wife, Vivien, although of a modestly aristocratic family, was too often vulgar—exposing her feelings and emotions spontaneously and inappropriately. People resented being unwilling witnesses to her outbursts. On the other hand, Tom knew that their discomfort with her also engendered a deeper sympathy for him, and what they perceived as his suffering was cause for their tender concern for him.

Tom had to admit to himself that he came to depend on Vivien as part of his presentation of himself to others. It was his "mask" to prevent others from getting too close: her often outrageous behavior made him seem long-suffering, patient, compassionate, and a bit pitiful. They would whisper among themselves that *anything* he could accomplish under such circumstances was certainly heroic. That suited Tom just fine.

Just before Christmas, at one of their sessions, Vittoz introduced Tom to a variation on his technique. Instead of picturing equations, symbols, or words to mentally create, Vittoz told Tom to choose those equations, symbols, or words that vexed him ("a formula that you perhaps do not understand or cannot solve," Vittoz said) and mentally erase them slowly, bit by bit, letter by letter.

At first, this exercise caused Tom some pain. Vittoz even remarked, "There is a heavy throbbing in your temples, Mr. Eliot." Unconsciously, Tom began to wring his hands. Vittoz held Tom's head steady for a moment. "Control yourself," he ordered.

Tom took a deep breath. Not wanting to reveal his discomfort, he sat on his hands. Another deep breath, then in his mind, he saw the handwritten word 'Vivien." Slowly, with an imagined brush, he began to wipe away her name stroke by stroke, starting at the end and working back towards the letter V. At first, his heart beat furiously. Then, with each difficult erasure, the beating subsided a little more and more. By the time he was able to erase all of her name, his jaw ached; he yawned greedily, his mouth opening to almost splitting.

Vittoz placed his hands on Tom's shoulders. "Tension and stress escaping at last," he said.

Tom rubbed his eyes. "I think I will stay another week, Doctor," he said, smiling.

"Yes, it will be the successful completion of my therapy," Vittoz agreed.

To Tom, miraculously, the poem seemed to be writing itself. At Christmas, he cabled greetings to his mother, saying that he was "working on a poem, too." He was alone on Christmas Day but used the time to review what he had accomplished in his great poem: somewhere between 800 and 1000 lines written, edited, and rewritten. He knew it still needed the precise and incisive editing of his friend, Ezra, but he felt that he had completed this first draft successfully: a poem of five parts, a poem that merged memory with experience, past with present, classical with contemporary, an expression of humanity distilled with the self.

"I cannot tell you how grateful I am," Tom said to Vittoz at their final meeting.

"It is not gratitude I seek, only your continued health. You have now the tools, I assure you." Vittoz shook Tom's hand warmly.

"My thanks nonetheless," Tom said.

On December 31, 1922, Tom waited for the train to Paris, his valise packed even more tightly with the two hundred lines of poetry he had written in Lausanne. He was anxious to share the new work with Ezra and happy to be returning to Paris for a few weeks, where he could continue to speak French. He was, for now, neither happy nor worried about seeing Vivien again. She was his wife and an unwavering supporter of his talent as a poet; he required nothing more of her. When the train arrived and he boarded, he thought only once of Lottie, not yet decided if he would see her again on his return to London. As the train started its three-hundred-mile journey to Paris, Tom looked up from his book. He whispered at the window, leaving the cloudy mist of his breath, "By the waters of Leman, I sat down. . . ." and he smiled.

1922

18. Preludes I

It was midmorning when Tom stepped onto the platform at Gare du Nord in Paris. "Hey, Possum!" a male voice called out clearly in English from the mixed din of metallic noises and French conversations. At five-ten, Ezra wasn't tall, but his bushy hair, combed back and up, gave him at least another inch so Tom could easily see him in the crowd of shorter Parisians.

"Ezra!" Tom called back and waved. He turned to the conductor, "*S'il vous plait, apporte ma valise ici*," and handed the man a ticket and one franc. "Ezra," he called again, "I need to wait here for my bag." He put out his arms to hug his friend warmly. "Is Dorothy with you? Vivien?"

Ezra shook his head. "Wimmen," he said laughing, "who needs 'em?" He pumped Tom's hand warmly.

But—" Tom looked around again, hoping that Ezra was joking.

"No, Tom, they really ain't here." He coaxed a smile from Tom. "But Rabbit iz here. Wut else duz you need?" Ezra persisted in his Brer Rabbit voice. "Get yer suitcase, and let's have a drink, shall we?"

In the café next to the station, Tom and Ezra settled at a small table. Ezra ordered two French 75s, telling Tom, "It's the latest rage in Paris, especially for us Americans celebrating Prohibition."

"What in blazes is it, Rabbit?" Tom asked when the pale drinks were deposited in front of them in tall champagne glasses.

"It's called a French 75 because it's got the kick of a French 75mm artillery gun. A simple concoction: mostly gin, your favorite, along with some syrup and some champagne."

Tom smacked his lips. "More for a woman, Ezra. I'd prefer the gin alone." Nevertheless, Tom emptied his glass. "Where's Viv? I sent her a cable."

Ezra finished his drink and signaled for two more. "She sent me, Tom. She said she was feeling poorly, so I left Dorothy with her at the hotel."

"Is she all right?" Tom asked; it would just be, he thought, more of the same.

Ezra shook his head. "No, she's moved to the Bon Lafontaine just next door. Said she liked the room better." Ezra poked Tom. "Tell me you've got more poetry for me, Possum."

"A great deal more, Ezra. Lausanne did wonders for me. Between what you've already seen and what I have revised and created, I've got the long poem I've wanted to write for years."

"And you're willing to let me take a scalpel to it as needed?" Ezra asked hopefully.

"Of course! As always, your edits and Viv's reactions are invaluable to me." Tom gulped half of his cocktail. "But I can't stay long, Ezra. I've got the possibility of an editorship waiting in London, a new literary magazine if I can pull it off."

"But how are you feeling, Tom, really?" Ezra touched Tom's sleeve.

"I'm healthy. Changed. Really, Ezra, I've done what you ordered: everything for the poem. In addition," he said, "just as I've changed, so has the poem's title."

Ezra squinted at Tom. "Not one of my suggestions, but before you spring the new title on me, tell me why." He polished off his drink with obvious relish.

"I was thinking of the Arthurian legends, especially as they are discussed in Miss Weston's book, *From Ritual To Romance*. I'm going to call the poem 'The Waste Land' a far more suitable title, I think."

Ezra smiled. "We'll see, Possum, we'll see."

When Tom arrived at the hotel, Vivien was sitting up in bed reading. "Come give us a kiss after long last," she said, holding out her arms.

Tom managed to give Viv only a quick kiss on her forehead. "No use to both of us getting sick. The influenza is still quite bad, Viv."

Vivien looked at Tom with disappointment while he turned away and started to unpack his valise. Then, with a false smile, she said, "Yes, Scofield had the same concern when he was here but saw it was unwarranted."

Tom's spine became rigid, but he did not turn around. "How is the fellow?" He continued taking clothes out of his suitcase. He was remembering Scofield: a scoundrel who, despite marriage to a beautiful, rich, and devoted wife, insisted on romancing every attractive woman in sight. Scofield called it 'free love.'

"Oh, the same, y'know, Tom," Vivien answered and sighed. "He was in Germany and invited me, but I didn't have the fare, so he agreed to come to Paris. I gave him our old room at the Calais and checked in here."

"I'm sorry I missed him," Tom said quietly.

"I was crushed, Tom, when you cabled that you were staying in Lausanne an extra week. Scofield was kind enough to keep me company in your absence."

Tom didn't hear the rest of Vivien's response; he was too busy imagining her name in his head and erasing it slowly but definitively letter by letter as Vittoz had taught him. When he was finished, he turned to her and smiled. "We'll head back to London mid-month, Vivien. I have much to do. Meanwhile, I'll be meeting with Ezra every day here in Paris to work on my poem."

"I'm glad that incredible poem will finally be done, Tom. And, if you don't mind, I think I'll stay on in Paris until the end of the month." She yawned.

"Will Scofield be returning?"

"No, but his cousin, Lucy, will be here. We'll find some activities to occupy us, I'm sure."

Tom tried to relax his shoulders. "Well, when I'm not working with Ezra, we can take in some shows at the music halls. Would you like that?"

Vivien clapped her hands in delight. "Oh, yes! It will be wonderful to go out and not be laid up in a hotel room day and night."

In Tom's mind flashed a quick vision of Vivien on her back in bed and a naked man approaching her, but this time, it was Scofield and not Bertrand Russell. Tom shook his head free of the image. "Yes, darling, I agree."

Later, dressing for dinner with James Joyce, Ezra Pound, and Ezra's American publisher, Horace Liveright, Tom realized that his imagined image of Viv with Scofield didn't upset him very much. Adultery seemed to mean so little to her, so perhaps he should follow her lead, he reasoned. And Lottie? He shrugged. It had become little more than a convenient arrangement.

At dinner Tom was introduced to Horace Liveright, one of the owners of the New York publishers Boni & Liveright. Horace had founded what he called the Modern Library, inexpensive reprints of European modernists. He was in Paris this winter looking for new authors.

Horace Liveright was only four years older than Tom but seemed older because of his no-nonsense business approach to life. Starting out selling bonds, he eventually decided on trying his hand at publishing once he had the backing of his father-in-law. Clean-shaven and handsomely dressed, he seemed overly assertive to Tom.

"So, you won't show it to me, eh?" Liveright asked for the third time as they were having after-dinner drinks.

Pound interjected, "Tom is still working on a few details. But, I promise you, it'll be a real feather in your cap."

"Still," the publisher insisted, "I can't meet your asking price of $200 in addition to the royalty. Besides, if you're telling the truth, the poem, even at its length, isn't enough for a book.

Would you add some notes at the end or a preface at the beginning?"

Tom started to shake his head, no, but Pound jumped in. "Listen, Horace, you've got the greatest novel of this century in Joyce's work, so why not also have the greatest poem of the century as well? We'll take $150, 15% royalty, and Tom'll think about adding some notes."

Horace pursed his lips. "All right," he said reluctantly. "For now, a gentleman's agreement, okay?"

Tom wanted the poem published, but he was reluctant to agree to providing notes, so the verbal 'contract' was preliminary at best. Nevertheless, he was excited that the poem (still not complete) already had a publisher in the States, and not just any publisher, but *Ezra Pound's* publisher!

Vivien did not see Tom off when he left for London on the sixteenth of January; she dined with him the night before, drank too much wine, and then complained all night and that morning of a terrible headache. Tom apologized that he could not delay his departure because he was scheduled to meet with Lady Rothmere in London, who was willing to fund a new literary journal under his editorship. He kept his suitcase by his side: it contained a number of pages of his poem that Ezra had reviewed.

Vivien had looked at the pages, making her own comments as well, mostly positive remarks on lines she particularly liked. In anticipation of his meeting with Lady Rothmere, she said, "I think, if it comes to pass, you should name your new journal *The Criterion*."

"Thank you, Viv, I like that."

In London, Tom made sure to ring up Virginia Woolf right away. She seemed glad to hear from him and immediately invited him to dinner the following night. He also called the bank to confirm that he would be at his desk soon, healthy and anxious to get back to work. Then, he spent the rest of the day and evening contemplating Ezra's extensive comments and suggestions. He enjoyed the quiet and familiarity of the empty apartment. Yet, by that night, he had come down with the flu and had to delay both his return to work and his visit to the Woolfs. However, he was content: Vivien was not due back for a week, so Tom had time to work on his poem as well as to see Lottie; he sent a note round to her by messenger inviting her to his apartment, enclosing a 2£ note for her cab fare.

He wrote to Scofield Thayer from his sickbed, not mentioning Paris or Vivien, but asking if Thayer's American publication, *The Dial*, would be interested in having exclusive printing for his long poem, "about four hundred and fifty words, in four parts," and enquiring about how much Scofield would pay. Tom hoped to be offered at least 50£ for the poem he'd worked on for over a year. Meanwhile, he continued, in correspondence, to discuss edits of *The Waste Land* with Ezra.

Each night of that week, with Vivien still in Europe, Lottie appeared at Tom's door at nine and left promptly at eleven, taking a cab back to Hogarth House. Each night, she watched him at his dining room table working on his poem for almost an hour, sometimes listening as he read lines aloud to her, sometimes just watching him edit pages with a pen or create ideas on his typewriter, a machine she'd never seen before.

"It makes an awful racket, that thing of yours," she remarked.

"But it's so much easier to use than a pen, Lottie," Tom explained. Pressing the keys takes time, so I can think and revise as I go."

"Ain't very useful for someone like me," she concluded.

Tom laughed. When he had worked an hour—he checked his watch to keep abreast of the time—he would set aside his papers and take Lottie's hands, help her to stand, and lead her to his bed. Each night, as he made love to her, he would say that he loved her, and, afterwards, lay beside her humming a tune or speaking of his childhood summers in Gloucester, Massachusetts. He never asked about her, never required anything more of her than to submit to his gentle seductions and listen to him in the dark room. At eleven, he would get up, put on a robe, help her to dress, and kiss her briefly at his door, saying, "See you tomorrow."

On the last night before Vivien was due to arrive, when Tom was about to send Lottie home, he embraced her for a long moment and said, "You have been a wonderful part of my healing, Lottie. I shan't forget that, not ever."

"We won't meet again, will we," Lottie said. It wasn't a question but her understanding. She was sad but not particularly upset; she had assumed this kind of ending from the first. After all, he had not asked much about her and never spoke of the future. By this time, she thought of him as a gentle lover but nothing more.

"Not like this, no." Tom held her close against his chest. He did not want her to look into his eyes. "You must leave me now, Lottie, for good. I hope you have learned from me what it means to be loved, and you must not settle for anything less in your life."

"I once wished we could marry—" she surprised herself by blurting out. She immediately regretted it because she loved him and did not want to disappoint him by being the kind of woman he wanted nothing to do with.

Tom put his hand on her mouth. "It was, is, never possible. Nor desirable, Lottie. I am not fit to be a husband, I've learned. Move forward, now, dear." He nudged her over the threshold, smiled, and closed the door.

At first, he thought he might weep for her and himself, but he realized that he had neither the need nor the desire to do so. He had not deceived the girl. He had promised nothing. He would always feel some affection for her—he had told her as much—but the relationship had run its course and had no place in the life of Tom Eliot, who emerged from Lausanne with his greatest creative effort fairly completed and his health much less in jeopardy.

There were still physical relapses, however; indeed, when Vivien returned to London on the twenty-fifth, she found him bedridden and quite irritable. He knew it was irrational, but he blamed Vivien for his extended illness because she had stayed on in Paris. Had she returned to London with him, he decided, he would not have been sick for so long. He needed to get back to work at the bank as well as to more actively seek out publishers for his reviews to earn money.

19. Preludes II

More than a week later, it was Lottie who opened the door of Hogarth House. She blushed when she saw him. "You look tired," she whispered and took his hat and coat.

He squeezed her elbow. "I'll be fine, Lottie." He hesitated, then added, "I hope you are the same." He quickly turned to the drawing room. "Hello, all!" he said brightly. "I've returned from my travails." He stood in the doorway, noting that, besides Virginia and Leonard, present were Mary Hutchinson and Clive Bell. They all clapped when they saw him, and Leonard immediately poured him a drink.

"Blast it, man!" Clive muttered. "Is it 'travels' or 'travails'? You are always twisting words *and* my brain."

"A little of both, Clive." Tom laughed. "I'm sorry that Vivien—" he started, taking the drink from Leonard.

"Yes, yes, as long as you're here, dear Tom," Virginia said, shaking her head. "You need not make excuses for her any longer." She thought he looked better but still taut and drawn tight like a violin string about to snap.

Mary patted the cushion beside her. "Sit here next to me," she coaxed. "You can use the warmth of friendship."

"I'm much better," Tom said, "although I've missed you all." He lowered himself into the place next to Mary.

She rubbed his arm vigorously. "Gad, you need loosening!"

Tom laughed uncomfortably. "Enough, Mary, please! If you must massage someone, do it with Clive." He rubbed his chin.

"And what's this?" Mary asked, touching the collar of his shirt.

"Ah, Paris converted me," Tom answered. "Shirts with sewn-in soft collars are all the rage now. No more starched collars, chafed necks, and abrasions. In a month or so, you'll all be wearing this style," he said, looking at Leonard and Clive.

"Looks quite comfortable," Leonard remarked. "I won't mind."

"Makes you look less stark and forbidding," Virginia said. "Softer."

"Rather proletarian, if you ask me," Mary sniffed.

"I hope to maintain being attractive," Tom said, laughing, "without becoming pathetic."

They all joined him in laughter, but the look in Virginia's eyes was unmistakable to Tom. He knew that she was concerned about him, seeing in him much of herself: often tired of life, isolated even when surrounded by friends, too acutely aware that the world was a dreary place.

"Pardon me, I've got to use the loo," Tom said, standing up.

Mary laughed. "Oh, Tom," she said, slapping her knee, "when you say it, you give it a French accent!"

"Well," Tom answered, "it is, after all, *l'eau*, ain't it?"

In the hall, he caught Lottie standing just inside the entryway to the stairs leading down to the kitchen. "Lottie!" he whispered, ducking into the shadow beside her. "My dear! I've thought of you often." He put his hand on her shoulder.

Lottie shrugged him off. "Thinkin' ain't doin', innit?" she answered coldly.

Tom tried to embrace her. "I thought you understood."

"I do now, Possum. I just want you to know that I'm fine. I've overheard the ladies talkin' about how they'd fall for you if you wanted, so I think myself lucky that I'd had you when they ain't. I wanted you to know that." Standing on tiptoe, she kissed his cheek, smiled, and ran down the steps.

Tom returned to the salon to Mary, saying, "There is finally some color returning to your cheeks, Tom. Is it only that you are constipated and need a diuretic?" She smiled.

"Would that were the solution to all my problems," Tom answered, but he blushed. He was still uncomfortable with such references. But more, he was trying to process Lottie's comments and that last chaste kiss she deposited on his cheek, which burned like a secret sin.

"You are sometimes such a mystery. If I were younger, Tom, I think I might fall in love with you," Virginia said. She smiled at Leonard. "But I am fortunate to have found Leonard instead."

"And I am equally fortunate," Tom answered, "that my upbringing and religion forbid me from pursuing you, a happily married woman." He turned to Mary and Clive. "You two are fortunate not to be slaves to convention as I am."

"Perhaps, Tom, you have just not found real love," Clive observed, putting his arm around Mary.

By late February, Vivien was in a nursing home outside of London, per doctor's orders, for at least three weeks. It was a relief to Tom because he could devote his time to launching the magazine that Lady Rothmere would fund. Still negotiating with her regarding his salary as well as editorial responsibilities and privileges, he was also asking other writers to commit articles and creative work to the journal. In general, his friendship and literary standing was sufficient to convince them, all except his dear friend, Ezra.

Tom heard from Scofield Thayer that he would offer only 35£ for *The Waste Land*, and Tom responded with a curt letter of refusal, saying, "You have asked me several times to give you the first refusal of any new work of mine, and I gave you the first refusal of this poem." He was angry, having heard that Scofield offered someone else more for a short story even though Eliot had worked on his poem for over a year. The matter was left to Ezra Pound, who insisted on trying to solve the problem.

Pound agreed that he would help out his friend in regard to the new journal, but he imposed a long list of conditions, most of which were connected to Pound's insistence that Tom be guaranteed a generous salary for his work. He finally agreed to contribute something, but not for the premier issue of *The Criterion*.

One June night, Tom surprised the Woolfs, as well as Mary Hutchinson and Clive, with a reading of his poem because even though he was still working on it, he wanted to see their reactions. His impression was that they were startled by the poem; they admired it although, he could sense, they did not completely understand it.

She had said nothing and only nodded, but Virginia was awestruck. She'd watched Tom, usually so cool and diffident, read the poem with an animation she did not know he possessed. *Possessed*, she thought, that was the word that described him.

When he was leaving, he told Virginia and Leonard that the poem was "quite finished. I've circulated it only to friends, and so far, reactions have been generally favorable."

"Are you asking if we will publish it, Tom?" Virginia said bluntly.

"No, no, Virginia," Tom protested. "Not yet. It's quite a long poem, but not long enough to be a book, I fear. An American publisher whom I'd met in Paris has tentatively offered to publish it if I can make it book-length."

"You mean to add to it?" Virginia asked.

"No, I think the poem is quite done as is. However, the fellow suggested that I add notes."

Virginia snorted. "To explicate your own work?" She added hastily, "We would publish it without such additions."

"Well, just to note the allusions, I think." Tom had not, in fact, started or, for that matter, even planned such notes.

Virginia shook her head. "And the poem is too long for journal publication?"

"I don't know." Tom shrugged. "We'll see. I'm still hoping *The Dial* will publish it first in America. Scofield offered me too little, but Ezra is hectoring him for a better deal. I would like the poem's publishing debut to occur simultaneously in America and London. As for your offer, Virginia, my answer is yes, but first, let me settle the other offers."

After Tom left, Virginia and Mary held hands as they talked quietly about Tom. "The poem is marvelous," Virginia said without jealousy.

"He let me read some parts of it previously. I think it is autobiographical," Mary proposed.

"If that is so," Virginia concluded, "then it is surely a long cry of anguish."

When he arrived home, he found Vivien sitting up waiting for him. "So, how are your friends?" she asked, her tone indicating she didn't much care.

"The same. They show concern for me, and they seem to have enjoyed my poem."

"It is no wonder regarding the poem. It's wonderful, Tom, your best work. As for your health, you know you must take better care of yourself. Else, who will minister to me when I am laid up?" Vivien chuckled, and Tom thought she sounded like a hunter who'd just trapped a helpless rabbit in a snare.

Tom spent a great deal of time discussing the yet-to-be published magazine, *The Criterion*, with Lady Rothmere, continuing his work at the bank and enduring, largely with indifference, his marriage to Vivien. He had come to tolerate her, so there were few arguments and upsets.

Sometimes, particularly when he visited the Woolfs, he thought of Lottie. He was so proud of her: she treated him no differently from the other gentlemen who called at the Woolf household—with a servant's deference and respect. Once, not able to help himself, he whispered to her as she was taking his hat and coat, "Lottie, you are such a wonderful girl!" but she only looked blankly at him and mumbled, "Thank you, Mr. Eliot", before disappearing.

When summer came, and what seemed to be (to everyone's relief) an end of the influenza, Pound notified Tom that Scofield had tentatively agreed to publish *The Waste Land* in the Fall or early Winter with a payment to Tom of the original 35£ but with an additional 450£ as a cash prize for the poem being announced as *The Dial's* 1922 award winner as best literary work. Tom needed only to hear from Horace Liveright that, as long as Tom would provide some pages of "Notes," *The Waste Land* would definitely be published in America in book form before the end of the year.

It was now only a matter of months when Tom would see what he said was his "best work" in print in America and, he planned, in London when he included "The Waste Land" in the premier issue of his *The Criterion*. He had no time to think of Lottie.

20: Transition

Feeling more confident of his status as a recognized poet, Tom worked diligently to make *The Criterion* a success. He spent much of his free time soliciting articles for the quarterly magazine; this often required him to accept invitations that he otherwise would have declined.

One such invitation was from someone Tom and Vivien had known for some years, Lady Ottoline Morrell. An artist and society hostess, Lady Ottoline was more than ten years Tom's senior, but she had a fondness for him as well as for Vivien and invited them often to her various parties and outings. She had met the Eliots through Bertrand Russell, who was her on-again, off-again lover for five years. She and her husband Philip had an open marriage, and Ottoline cared for the several children that her husband had produced in his extramarital affairs.

She maintained homes both in London and Garsington Manor, near Oxford. The Oxford house was considered a retreat for the many artists and writers who Ottoline encouraged, and it was even, during World War I, a haven for pacifists and conscientious objectors.

Tom and Vivien arrived at Garsington Manor late. It was clear to Ottoline that the two had been arguing because they pointedly greeted the others while turning their backs on each other. Being late, they were immediately ushered into the dining room with everyone else. His name card indicated that Tom was to be seated across from Vivien rather than next to her. He thought this unusual, but he was relieved at its convenience: he and Viv had argued heatedly in the cab, and he was glad to not be sitting next to her during the meal. He introduced himself to the woman on his right. "How do you do? I'm Thomas Eliot."

"I know exactly who you are and I've been wanting to meet you since your wonderful poem 'Prufrock.' I hope you don't mind that I swapped Julian Huxley's name card with yours. He's such a dreadful bore." The woman was attractive in a dazzling way: heavy black kohl around her eyes, almost ghostly white makeup, and blood-red lipstick. Her arms were ringed from wrist to elbow with numerous wooden bracelets. She spoke with a slight French accent.

"I'm sorry. I'm afraid I don't know you. But thank you in regard to my poetry." Tom bowed his head. He felt his ears turning red and getting hot; the woman's aggressive femininity bothered him. He felt nauseous.

"I'm Nancy Cunard. My mother—sitting over there—" she waved her hand vaguely to her right, "is American and divorced from my father, Bache Cunard. I'm sure you've sailed on his liners."

Tom signaled for one of the footmen. "Bring me a whiskey, old man." He needed a drink. Turning from Nancy, he said to Viv across the table, "Everything fine, darling?"

At first, Vivien looked sternly at him; the argument they'd had on the way here was still fresh in her mind. But when she saw Nancy Cunard put her hand on Tom's sleeve, Vivien smiled and said, "Who's the beautiful woman next to you, dear?"

"This is Nancy Cunard, Viv." He turned to Nancy. "That's my wife, Vivien Haigh-Wood." When the footman placed the whiskey in front of him, Tom picked up the glass as if toasting Viv and emptied it in one gulp. "Another, please," he immediately said to the footman. Seeing Viv's jealousy developing, he purposely stretched his arm onto the back of Nancy's chair and smiled.

Tonight, Tom took a particularly perverse pleasure in provoking Vivien, and he could not have done it so well without the unwitting assistance of Nancy Cunard or a great deal of whiskey. So, at dinner, he continued to encourage Nancy's flirtations with him, all the while keeping one eye on Vivien across the table who alternated between a sullen petulance and a shrill but clearly artificial indifference to him.

Vivien tried to match Tom's whiskey intake; as a result, and because of her physical delicacy, she was inebriated sooner. As she spoke, her speech getting sloppier by the moment, the odor of the whiskey on her breath seemed to spread and then mix, unpleasantly, with the pungent smell of the ether she had been prescribed and in which she over-indulged to dull her physical pains and mental depressions. She also tried to match Tom's flirtations with Nancy by throwing herself at the hapless Julian Huxley.

Each time that Tom leaned in towards Nancy (who obliged with mutual interest), Vivien would mimic his action or invent one of her own: touch Julian's arm, briefly lean her head on his shoulder, or familiarly push a lock of his hair back from his forehead. Before long, Julian, awkward and embarrassed, turned to the older woman on his other side to engage in animated conversation with her and ignore, as much as possible, the more unpredictable Vivien.

When dinner was over, and the guests retired to the parlor for light conversation, both Tom and Vivien found themselves well on their way to drunkenness, unsteady on their feet and bleary-eyed. "Tom, do sit here," said Nancy, patting the cushion beside her on the sofa. She held her liquor much better than Tom.

"Don't mind if I do," said Tom, dropping gracelessly to the seat beside Nancy. He smiled at her. "Tell me again why you like my poetry." He had left his wife, Vivien, standing in the middle of the room.

"How can she when she hardly knows you," Vivien said loudly, her hands on her hips. "Others can barely understand you, Tom. Only I, your wife, understand." Vivien's voice was strident, cutting through the conversations in the room. Everyone was silent for a moment.

"Oh, dear Vivien, come sit here and tell me about your recent trip to Paris," Ottoline said quickly, taking Vivien's arm and leading her to a chair across the room. She smiled at everyone, her way of assuring her guests that she had everything under control. From out of her sleeve, she snapped open a small fan and waved it rapidly to dispel the ether odor that wafted unpleasantly from Vivien. "Or, perhaps, dear," Ottoline suggested, "we can sit a moment in the garden to enjoy the night sky."

Tom jumped up to take Vivien's arm. He felt slightly dizzy, realizing he'd drunk too much. "Thank you, Lady Ottoline," he said formally and with studied care, "I believe Viv and I would enjoy a turn in your garden." He led Vivien, who now leaned into him possessively, to the French doors leading out back. As he walked Viv into the dark night, he heard murmurs of sympathetic disapproval from the room.

Garsington's backyard was large and carefully manicured. Part of the lawn was given over to a jumble of small tables and chairs where guests could converse or rest in the fresh air day or night. In the dark, Tom had to carefully maneuver himself and Viv over the uneven terrain to the group of chairs. He sat Viv firmly onto one of the seats and lowered himself onto another next to her. "Viv, you've made a fool of yourself," he said.

"And, of course, you bloody disapprove."

"So, shall we continue our disagreement from earlier?" Tom sneered. He knew that speaking calmly and confidently heightened Vivien's fury and, right now, that amused him.

"You're a bloodless serpent, Tom. You take great pleasure in hurting me, I think."

"Nonsense, Viv. I'm the one who is most hurt. You drank too much tonight, on top of having had too much ether before we left the house." Tom made no move to comfort her or even look at her. He sat in the chair staring up at the stars. "I will have to spend the next few days apologizing to everyone for your behavior."

"And to Nancy Cunard?" Vivien asked.

"Yes, to her as well. Not only did she witness your untoward behavior, but she could not help but realize that she was the target of much of your ire."

"Not without cause," Viv insisted.

Tom shook his head but, realizing that Vivien could not see him do so, said in denial, "You're being unreasonable." The fresh air was, he realized, dispelling his drunkenness. He took a deep breath. "You know me better than that, Viv."

"Sometimes, I think I know you hardly at all, Tom," Vivien answered and fell silent.

They sat without speaking for a while. The dark around them—the sky filled with stars that were too far away to shed light, earth rich and black with natural life that was now somnolent at night—was simply a reflection of the dark between them. They'd married too hastily. They'd misjudged one another's desires and needs. There was only one thing they had in common: an aspiration for Tom's success, and it kept them together.

Now, however, Tom seems to be close to achieving that goal, and its attainment would mean the end of their mutual objective. Tom knew this, but he also knew that Vivien would never acknowledge it. She had no ambition for herself, only for him. It was an incredible selflessness that he appreciated yet resented because it seemed to him that such surrender of the self was almost divine, and Vivien's expression of it for him was somehow carnal and debased its spirituality. He hated that Vivien could act in a way of which he was, himself, incapable.

Vivien's voice rose softly out of the dark. "Tom, did you love me? Do you love me now? Will you ever love me?"

"I thought I did," he answered.

"And?" Vivien was not satisfied with his response.

Tom said nothing more. An invisible insect buzzed near his head. He waved it away with his hand in the same way that his silence hoped to wave away Vivien's question.

"You know," she said, her voice suddenly clear and strong, "that Nancy Cunard will suck you dry, Tom, drink up all your poetry like a vampire, and leave you empty."

Tom thought Viv sounded sober now, drained at least of the alcohol, if not also of the ether. "I might enjoy that for a change, Viv," he answered cruelly. "It might be nice to be with a woman who appreciates what I can do for her. Besides, at least as far as the poetry goes, I've done my best work. There won't be anything there again for a while, I'd guess."

Vivien sighed. "I'm certain of it, Tom, you will be seduced by her given the opportunity."

"Hardly, Viv," Tom replied and stood up. "I choose chastity as the nobler path." He had decided that his affair with Lottie had proved his sexual potency; he needed nothing more. "Shall we give our farewells to everyone and head home?"

"What you choose and what your vanity dictates are not always the same," Vivien warned and took his arm. "The night air has made me disappointingly clear-headed."

21. Interlude: Nancy Cunard

It was Vivien who noticed how popular he had become. "Oh, you must go without me again, darling," Vivien insisted, self-pity dripping from her voice as she lay in bed, their little pet Yorkie fast asleep and pressed against her hip.

"I hate leaving you alone, Viv," Tom answered, then added, "Although that pup won't ever allow you to be alone, I'll wager." He was sitting on the far edge of the bed.

"I rather like the affection," Vivien said, her meaning clearly, to Tom, more than a simple reference to dogs.

"It's a matter of temperament, I suppose," Tom mused. "My preference will always be for the mysterious feline." He stood up, straightening his black tie before buttoning his dinner jacket; he'd been told the party required formal dress. "I'll give your regrets to Emerald, of course." He was referring to Maud Burke, the former wife of Sir Bache Cunard and the mother of one of their acquaintances, Nancy Cunard.

"But be sure to avoid Nancy, dear Tom, she's been sniffing after you for quite some time." Vivien sighed. She'd heard lots of stories about Nancy's predatory designs on men, and she didn't want Tom to be one of her conquests. "Remember the Lady Morrell's dinner party? When was that? I can't remember. She fell all over you, gushing about your Prufrock poem? And you sloshed to the gills, led her on. Don't think I didn't see you, darling."

Tom blushed but insisted, "I don't remember any of that, Viv."

"Oh, yes, it happened. But I wasn't a bit alarmed. After all, I know you, Tom. All words and little action, as it were." Absently, she ran her fingers slowly through her hair as if catching ideas. "I don't doubt she'll seek you out tonight. You must insist that I'm there with you, just temporarily separated in the crowd." Vivien was enjoying her imagined ruse.

"I shan't connect with her, Viv, I promise." Tom said dutifully, but he was enjoying hearing that he was desired by one of the most scandalously precocious women in London; he shivered imperceptibly. He had remained chaste since breaking it off with Lottie, so this observation of Vivien's titillated him.

The party had the ostensible purpose of celebrating the discovery of a jazz band newly arrived from America by Lady Cunard, Nancy's mother, who in boredom had insisted that everyone now call her Maud, or "Emerald," Burke. Tom knew nothing about the musicians; he'd been given what he called a "second- or third-hand" invitation by Mary Hutchinson, who had herself been invited by her lover, Clive Bell. Mary insisted that Tom must attend with some of his poetry in hand because there were guests who could further his career—or, at least, his reputation—as an international poet. Tom arrived at The Eiffel Tower Hotel and Restaurant in Soho at nine, relieved to see some of his acquaintances already there—Mary, Clive, and Wyndham Lewis—but dismayed by the greater number of strangers; still, he put on his best face and nodded politely to people.

The owner of The Eiffel Tower, Rudolph Stulik, shrewdly decided to encourage the rich of London to patronize his place after Nancy Cunard had discovered it during one of her alcohol-fueled jaunts with some of the artists and writers of Soho; she'd convinced her mother that this place was perfect: food more palatable and continental than the usual London fare, a neighborhood that was not strict about morals, and discreet rooms upstairs. Emerald loved the implied naughtiness, and soon, she and her social set had essentially adopted the place, thereby sending the less-wealthy artistic patrons elsewhere.

Before long, Mary and Clive disappeared, probably off to Virginia's house in Richmond, and Wyndham, his wife home alone, eyed some of the women to leave Tom to fend for himself. Suddenly overcome with shyness in the crowd, Tom eased his way toward the exit.

Stulik was standing there, a cigar in hand, looking up at the night sky. "Too much, eh?" he said to Tom, who was fiddling with his wing collar and bow tie.

"A bit stuffy. Too many people," Tom said.

"*Jah*. You look like a nice young gentleman. Go upstairs and relax for a moment in one of the rooms. There's whiskey in all of 'em." Stulik smiled amiably, then turned back to staring at the sky.

Tom hesitated, then mumbled, "Thanks." He wanted some time to decide how to present himself to these people. He climbed the stairs to the second floor.

The hallway was dimly lit and not very long. There were only three doors on either side, and four of the six were ajar, the light from each room spilling into the hallway. Two were closed; Tom assumed these were occupied. He walked to the far end of the hall and entered the empty room on the left.

It was furnished simply: a bed, nightstand, a small table, lamp, and two chairs. The curtain on the window, a dark damask, was pulled tight across the frame. Tom sat in one of the chairs and poured himself a whiskey from the previously-opened bottle. He decided not to loosen his tie despite the fact that he could feel the chafing on his neck; he'd gotten used to the soft-collared shirts, so this stiff one irritated him. He would have to return downstairs to mingle. Instead, he stretched his neck backwards and let his head fall backwards. He closed his eyes.

The door opened. "So, here you are at last," a woman's voice said. She shut the door behind her. "Rudolph said you'd be up here; I just had to guess which room." Nancy laughed and sat down.

Tom jerked into a stiff, shoulders-straight position. "Sorry, I just wanted a bit of a respite."

"Nancy, darling, remember? My name's Nancy. I'm sure you know that I've been looking for you ever since you published that wonderful Prufrock poem."

Tom looked at Nancy Cunard with surprise. Her impossibly slim, lithe body reminded him of Sarah Bernhardt: attractive in a highly sexual way. He blushed. "Thank you for the compliment, but that poem was written by the person I no longer am."

"Then let's drink to whomever you are now, Mr. Eliot. Or should I call you Thomas?" She pronounced his name with a French accent, so it sounded like *Toe-mahss*. Nancy poured herself a drink and topped off Tom's.

They talked about poetry, then London, and then Paris. They drank until the bottle was empty. Nancy went to the door and shouted: "Rudolph, more whiskey, please. *Vite!*" and when Stulik knocked and delivered the bottle, Nancy locked the door behind him. After putting the whiskey on the table, she sat on the floor at Tom's feet and folded her arms in his lap. "Tell me more about the person you are now, Mr. Thomas Eliot."

When Tom found his watch in the heap of clothes on the floor, it was three a.m. He could still hear some voices below, but mostly hushed, as if a few people were quietly chatting. While he was dressing, Nancy woke and, propping herself on an elbow, laughed. "We really should have done this in bed, Thomas. My back would have preferred it."

"I'm afraid I was not acting the gentleman," Tom answered, buttoning his shirt. He'd managed to put on his trousers, but his socks, shoes, and dinner jacket still lay on the floor, jumbled with Nancy's clothes. He would not look at her; she'd pulled a cover from the bed to wrap around herself.

"Certainly, we're not done," she purred. "We haven't emptied the second bottle yet." She stretched out on the floor where they'd made love. "Let's use the bed this time, dear."

Tom hesitated. He needed only to put on his socks and shoes and fold his dinner jacket over his arm to be ready for his departure. He looked at Nancy and thought of Vivien. They had the same eyes: huge, doe-like, and somehow haunted as if the world were in hot pursuit in order to castigate her for some awful wrong. His hands itched with a memory of Lottie's body. His heart melted, and his body became invigorated. "Gladly," he said assertively. As he pressed his lips to hers, he thought he should recite to her some of his new long poem because he was sure it would seduce her as surely as she had seduced him that night. Fleetingly, as she pulled him aggressively toward her, he remembered his references to Lady Fresca in his poetry, and he smiled sardonically.

When Tom arrived home at six a.m., Ellen was already in the kitchen preparing tea and laying out biscuits. He nodded to her before going into the bedroom to retrieve fresh clothes. Vivien was asleep, curled in on herself as usual, looking like a forlorn child. Tom heaped a new set of clothes and his shaving kit into his arms and slipped out to the dining room. "Give me a basin, Ellen," he called to their maid in the kitchen, and when she appeared with the steamy water and a towel, he thanked her and ushered her back into the kitchen. "I'll just be a moment," he said, closing the door between the two rooms.

While he shaved, from which he derived physical pleasure and comfort, he looked at himself in the mirror and smiled. Nancy was voracious, he thought, but so delicious. The whiskey had given him liquid courage. He knew: a shedding of inhibitions so that he indulged his fantasies about making love. He did what he wanted, used her for his own pleasure, exhausted her, then with renewed energy excited her, aroused her, victoriously overwhelmed her until she clung to him in surrender.

"Tom?" Vivien's voice called weakly from the bedroom.

Tom cleaned up his shaving materials and opened the door to the kitchen. "Ellen, please take care of these things," he said, pointing to the basin and the pile of clothes from last night on the table. He headed to the bedroom.

"Hello, Viv," he said brightly. "Are you feeling better?"

"Yes, Tom, but I'm afraid my medicines knocked me out. I fell asleep so early before you got home. How was the party?" Dinah, the Yorkie, was still curled up beside her.

"Oh, the usual," Tom said, shrugging his shoulders. "I stayed quite late because there were so many people interested in my poetry. I was asked to read something, but I declined. That audience wasn't quite right for my writing, I think. However, there was an excellent jazz band playing—they just recently arrived from America—and I was able to chat with

Clive and Mary for a bit." Tom patted Vivien's hand, reassuring her of the party's usefulness to his career.

"And did you speak to Emerald?" Vivien asked.

"I'm afraid I could never get quite near her enough. It was such a crush in that place. Oh, when you're better, we'll have to dine there one evening. It's quite a charming place."

"But Emerald will think I was snubbing her!" Vivien cried in dismay.

"No, no, I bumped into her daughter, Nancy, who promised to convey your regrets to her mother."

"You saw Nancy? You spoke with her?" Vivien's voice grew panicked.

"Yes, she's quite harmless, Viv," Tom reassured his wife, again patting her hand. "I absolutely controlled her." He remembered how powerful he'd felt over Nancy. He thought it should have been that way with Vivien on their wedding night or later, after she'd been with Bertrand Russell.

Vivien sighed. "I wish I could have been there to see it, Tom. I've heard that Nancy is quite the man-eater. I would have worried horribly if I thought you'd gotten caught in her clutches."

"I hope you know me better than that." Tom squeezed Vivien's shoulder. "Now, shall we have some breakfast? I'm positively famished."

22. Publication and Postlude

In 1922 and through much of 1923, Tom's preoccupation changed from creating *The Waste Land* to getting it distributed widely throughout the publishing world. He believed in himself and his poem, thanks in part to his cure and recuperation in Lausanne, but when he returned to London, some of his problems, unchanged, still waited for him: his wife continued to be a burden for which he felt no less responsible as the years passed, and his fortunes were still tenuous, necessitating not only his continuing to work at the bank, but also to continue lecturing, reviewing and editing for the needed income.

Scofield Thayer assured Tom that he would publish the poem in *The Dial* in New York. He called Tom from Germany to give him the news. "Tom, *The Dial* with your poem in it will be on the stands and in people's hands at the end of October even though the issue will be labeled as November 1922."

"That's wonderful news, Thayer, thanks."

"I'm glad we were able to solve our financial differences." Scofield was referring to the deal brokered by Ezra Pound and Tom's American advocate, the lawyer John Quinn. Tom was to receive the magazine's regular rate for poetry (despite the unusual length of *The Waste Land*) as well as another 475£ as the winner of the magazine's annual literary prize.

The magazine had started as a vehicle for the American Transcendental Movement in the mid-nineteenth century but folded because of financial instability. It was revived at the close of that century as a political review based on and reflecting Midwestern views. Again, falling on hard financial times, it was sold to a New Yorker who steered it to more liberal views. Eventually, it fell onto hard times again until one of the original investors, Scofield Thayer, with Dr. James Sibley Watson Jr., a friend from Harvard, bought it outright in 1920 and steered it to become a modernist literary magazine. In their first year of ownership, Thayer and Watson published William Butler Yeats' "The Second Coming."

The publication of *The Waste Land* in the premier issue of *The Criterion* in October 1922 was quickly followed at the end of the same month (although dated November 1922) in an issue of *The Dial* in New York. While Eliot's new magazine had only a small subscriber base at its inception, *The Dial* was well-known and widely respected. Magazine sales for that issue rose dramatically to almost five thousand and, for the following December issue, to over six thousand.

Tom had also decided to print the poem in his own magazine, *The Criterion*, in the same month. It was part of his plan to have the poem appear "worldwide" simultaneously.

However, Scofield Thayer took the insult. "Tom, I thought *The Dial* was going to have initial publishing rights."

"You did," Tom insisted. "No one else in America published the poem."

"But, you printed it in your own journal, *The Criterion*." Scofield was clearly upset.

"Which is basically local to London. I wanted simultaneous exposure on this side of the Atlantic," Tom replied affably.

"I think we disagree on the meaning of rights," Scofield answered.

They spoke after that but were distantly formal with one another. Scofield felt he had been used.

In December 1922, Boni & Liveright in New York published the book-length version of *The Waste Land*, a version with "Footnotes." The publishers used extreme spacing for the publication, thereby able to produce a book of sixty-four pages. Back in March 1922, Eliot had offered the British book publication to the Woolfs' Hogarth Press. It took more than a year later, but in September 1923, their version was released: 35 pages handset by Virginia and printed by Leonard. They produced 460 copies. It was more a pamphlet than a book, but Tom was more pleased with it than with the American edition, largely because they had maintained his specific line breaks and formatting. In addition, and probably most importantly, the

Woolfs had printed the poem as Eliot intended, without the "footnotes."

This had been Tom's plan all along: to have the poem published almost simultaneously in both the United States and Great Britain. Further, he used all his powers of persuasion, cajolery, and even some petty deception, to have the poem printed soon thereafter as a book. He was certain that this would cement his reputation as an important poet of the modern world.

The first appearances of the poem were met with mixed reactions. Tom, easily swayed by what he believed others thought of him, was alternately depressed and delighted by the reviews. The worst of them called the poem "modern ugliness," "a hodgepodge of grandeur and jargon," "a parade of pompous erudition," and, in attempts at cruel cleverness, "a waste paper." They complained of his overly-precise language, his erudition, and worst of all, some suggested the poem to be a hoax of "high-spirited spoofing."

The favorable reviews mostly recognized the poem as innovation representative of a new and exciting change in poetic subject and structure. These reviewers also noted Eliot's use of language and his erudition, but in positive and admirable terms.

It was interesting that reviews written by those who knew Eliot—some for many years—did not, whether out of respect or courtesy, mention his deep reliance on Ezra Pound's influence and editing. Tom himself had wrestled with whether to include a formal acknowledgement of Pound's role in the completion of the poem; Pound himself would not weigh in with an opinion and, finally, Tom decided to withhold that acknowledgement until a later printing.

Tom had, for years, insisted to his literary circle that genuine poetry was impersonal rather than personal, that it sought to expunge rather than expose the author, the poet. When "The Waste Land" was published in *The Criterion*, his friends would see in it their world—war and epidemic, class struggle and revolution, all the ills of a modern city like

London—but their world reimagined in its parallels to ancient times and classical literature, in its modern inventions of science, art, and music. "The Waste Land," they saw, was the sound of tectonic plates grinding perilously against one another; it was personal peril and despair written largely in historical terms. It was the whole world at once suffering Tom's breakdown.

When, just before Christmas in 1923, the Woolfs sent him his first copy of their printing of *The Waste Land*, Tom, now identifying himself as the editor of *The Criterion*, wrote them a warm letter praising their printing and indicating that it was their edition that he would send as complimentary copies to friends and reviewers. And, once he addressed the envelope to them at the Hogarth House Press, he thought of Lottie and knew that she, at long last, required a note of thanks as well. He was now confident that there was no need to be clandestine about his acquaintance (as he described it) with Lottie.

19 December 1923

My dearest Lottie,

I hope you will have seen, after this letter, how this infernal machine of mine, a typewriter, is a good thing insofar as it makes clear the words I need to tell you and which you need to always remember.

When I was with you were some of the happiest moments of my life, when my life was otherwise quite miserable. You were a shining light that I could turn to and be warmed by, a source of vitality to me, who was so malnourished of positive and uplifting emotions. But in that time of misery, I wrote my poetry inspired by that very desperation, and your love—my love for you—kept me from total failure, teetering on the brink (but not falling), until I could finally heal.

Now I am healed. I have completed the poem that was my dark shadow for years. It is published (whether, finally, to great acclaim or to ignominy, I do not know). You, dear Lottie, played your part in that process, but now the process is done.

I will always cherish the love we shared and the love you helped me to express. And I will always be grateful for your silence about us. That speaking out would ruin both our reputations goes without saying. More importantly, I have come to understand that I will be a better man only by my own actions. The first is for me to beseech you for your forgiveness if you believe I have injured you in some way. The second is for me to beseech God's forgiveness for my adulteries (yours in helpless love, others in vengeful lust). The third is for me to devote my life to purity. I am thinking that I no longer need a doctor but a minister to cure me.

Yours,

Tom

When the letter came to Hogarth House for Lottie, the butler, Mr. Higgins, was greatly upset. He separated the letter from the mail for the Woolfs and carried it downstairs as if it were a rabid animal. "And what is this?" he asked Cook, placing the letter on the servants' table.

Cook wiped her hands on her apron and peered down at the letter. It was addressed simply to 'Lottie – Hogarth House' with a return address from 'T.S. Eliot.' "Oh, my," Cook said, "has the upstairs seen it?"

"Do you think I would have been able to bring it down here if that were the case?" Higgins asked, clearly annoyed. "I hope you will sort this out." He rubbed his hands together as if washing away any responsibility. "And not a word to the Missus."

Cook nodded and placed the letter in her apron. She went back to her cooking, assuming there would be time after dinner to speak with Lottie.

And so there was. "Lottie, sit with me in the garden, would you? Bring a shawl against the chill."

The request was unusual, but Lottie welcomed a chat. She had been feeling particularly lonely because it was the Christmas season, and she had no family to celebrate with; she wasn't looking forward to spending the holidays serving the seemingly constant influx of guests at the Woolf household.

The two women sat under the cold December moon. There was no breeze, but the air was chill and made them catch their breath. "This came today. Higgins gave it to me," Cook said, placing the letter in Lottie's hand.

"A letter?" Lottie asked, squinting in the moonlight. When she peered closer, she recognized Tom's handwriting. He had visited the Woolfs only three or four times since she last saw him at his apartment, and he had not contacted her at all. When he'd visited the Woolfs, he was cordial to her and almost too formal, too polite. He seemed to have gone out of his way to make sure they would not accidentally meet anywhere in the house, and he always averted his eyes when they were in the same room.

"You've not seen 'im, 'ave you?" Cook asked quietly.

"No. We said our farewells." Lottie kept turning the envelope over in her hands.

"Did he break your heart, Lottie?" Cook touched Lottie's arm tenderly.

"Perhaps a little. But he was no scoundrel. We both knew from the start, Cook, that I was in service and would remain so for me whole life. I was foolish to think my station would ever change."

"Do you think that you and him would 'ave been 'appy?"

Lottie looked in Cook's eyes. The older woman was leading her to a conclusion she hadn't wanted to admit. But, here it was, after all. "No, Cook. When I was with him, he was wonderful but so fragile and weak. I think I made him feel stronger. But after he went to Switzerland, he came back stronger on his own, but not so. . . " Lottie searched for the right word.

"Not so *carin'*, I'd say," Cook surmised.

"Yes. It's as if he never needed *me* so much as he needed what I was." She bowed her head.

"And you was a young, innocent girl who did whatever he wanted," Cook concluded irritably. "So, here's a letter now. Do you think he wants you back?"

Lottie gave the letter back to Cook. "I've learned something, Cook. Being in service ain't so bad. I know where I stand. I know what I have to do every day. It's steady, and it's honest. The world outside is dangerous for the likes of me."

Cook stood up. "We'll catch a pneumonia out here. Come inside, and I'll find something sweet for us to have with tea before we go to bed."

Two weeks later, Tom's letter was returned to him with the message: "Refused. Return to Sender." Tom looked at the envelope, but he had already decided what to do. His conscience was clear: he had done his penance to Lottie, and it need not be shared with the world. He gently tossed the envelope into the small furnace, warming his room. There would be more poems, and what he shared with Lottie, too, would be "all for the poem."